FALLING FOR DALLAS

Other books by Carolynn Carey:

A Summer Sentence

FALLING FOR DALLAS

•

Carolynn Carey

AVALON BOOKS
NEW YORK

Published by Thomas Bouregy & Co., Inc.
160 Madison Avenue, New York, NY 10016

Library of Congress Cataloging-in-Publication Data

Carey, Carolynn.
    Falling for Dallas / Carolynn Carey.
       p. cm.
    ISBN 0-8034-9792-X (acid-free paper)
    1. Single mothers—Fiction.   2. Tennessee—Fiction.
I. Title.
    PS3603.A737F35 2006
    813'.6—dc22

                                            2006009969

PRINTED IN THE UNITED STATES OF AMERICA
ON ACID-FREE PAPER
BY HADDON CRAFTSMEN, BLOOMSBURG, PENNSYLVANIA

For my beloved nieces and nephews. They say what doesn't kill you makes you stronger. Thanks for all the strength you've given me. I love you all.

Many people have nurtured and supported my love of the written word over the years:

My parents, Iris and H.B. Lester, exemplified the value and joy to be found in books.

My brother and sisters always supported my zeal for learning.

My aunts, uncles, cousins, and in-laws taught me that roots run deep and live long.

My friends, both my fellow writers and my fellow readers, have shared their knowledge and enthusiasms with me.

My husband, Floyd, believed in me even when I told him I would never succeed.

And our daughter, Allison, will always be my most treasured inspiration.

Chapter One

He had arrived. The sign said so. Barbourville, Tennessee. Population 2,089.

Dallas Vance suppressed a sigh and eased his foot off the gas pedal. He didn't want a run-in with Horace Barnhart, the overly vigilant deputy who patrolled the roads around these parts.

And considering the fact that he'd drawn the short straw and was going to have to live in this tiny town for a few weeks, he didn't want to get off on the wrong foot with his nephew-in-law, the sheriff, either.

He touched his brake and slowed to a crawl in observance of the 25-mph speed limit. Easing down Kessler Boulevard, he glanced from one side of the street to the other. He had to admit

1

that Barbourville was a picturesque town. Towering maples—showing just a hint of yellow and orange—bordered the street, while well-preserved Victorian houses gradually gave way to businesses as he approached the downtown area, which bustled with activity as the noon hour approached.

Overall, however, the town appeared less crowded today than it had just a month ago when he'd visited the last time. No doubt the approach of fall had sent the summer residents and their children scampering back to their homes in nearby cities to prepare for the upcoming school year.

Dallas tapped his brakes again, then slowed to a full stop at the town's single traffic light. The McCray County Courthouse sat in a neat lawn to his right, and cattycornered across the street was the ever-popular Sonny's Diner. His gaze slid past the unpretentious eatery and settled on the storefront window of Beth Ann's Place, the clothing store owned by one of the few women Dallas had ever met who didn't soon reduce him to yawns.

A smile lifted the corners of his lips. On the couple of occasions he and Beth Ann had met, verbal sparring and less-than-subtle flirting had kept both of them on their toes even though they realized flirting was all there could ever be between them. Beth Ann made it clear that she was devoted to her son and their life in Barbourville, while Dallas couldn't imagine living anywhere but Chicago.

Still . . . a little harmless flirtation never hurt anybody.

Besides, he really needed to talk to Beth Ann, who was one of the few people in Barbourville who understood the relationship between him and Megan McCray, his late sister's only child. He needed advice, and he figured Beth Ann was the best person to give it.

After all, Beth Ann and Megan had become close friends last summer when Megan rented a room from Beth Ann. At that time Megan had told Beth Ann all about her overly protective uncles—the triplets from Chicago. Megan had explained that when Dayton, Denver, and Dallas were only ten years old, they had promised their beloved older sister on her deathbed that they would watch over her little girl. In the years that followed, taking care of Megan had become such an ingrained habit, they couldn't seem to let go even though she was now a grown woman with triplets of her own.

As Dallas recalled from last summer, Beth Ann had seemed to understand the brothers' intense need to look after Megan. He wasn't sure she approved, but at least she understood. Now maybe she would be willing to help him convince Megan to let him stay in Barbourville and help her with her beautiful little girls who were a little over a month old.

Logically, Dallas knew Megan could manage very well without him. But Dayton, the worrywart of the three brothers, had been fretting ever since he visited two weeks ago and found Megan looking tired and acting stressed. Dayton had returned to Chicago convinced that one of the brothers needed to return to Barbourville for a few weeks to help out, and because Dallas had the lightest workload at the time, he was elected. In the end, Dallas had given in so Dayton wouldn't feel obligated to come back himself.

The problem might be convincing Megan that she did in fact stand in need of his help.

When the traffic light turned green, Dallas eased down the street and into a parking space in front of Beth Ann's store. He shifted into park and sat for a moment, smiling to himself as he always did when he thought of Beth Ann. He seriously doubted that the woman had any idea of how beautiful she was, with her porcelain complexion, green eyes, and gorgeous red hair. She was bright, too, with a sharp wit that he found nearly irresistible.

His smile widened. He opened the car door

and stepped out onto the sidewalk. For the first time since he'd known he was coming to Barbourville, he was really looked forward to one aspect of the experience.

Beth Ann Stanfield sat back on her heels and rolled her shoulders in an effort to work the kinks out. She'd spent most of the morning on her knees behind the counter checking boxes of new merchandise for the upcoming winter, and she was not only tired, but she was pretty doggone hungry. Five more minutes, she promised herself, and she would break to eat the sandwich she'd brought from home.

The bell above her shop door jingled. "Please, God," she murmured, "let this be a customer instead of a creditor."

She pushed herself to her feet, dusting off the knees of her jeans as she stood, then shoved an errant strand of hair away from her face. She looked toward the door, blinked twice, and suppressed a moan.

Of course every pore in her body was screaming out a prodigious welcome at the spectacular sight of Dallas Vance walking into her store, but what law of nature decreed that she must always look her worse when he was around?

The first time they'd met, she'd been under

the mistaken impression that Dallas and his brothers had arrived in Barbourville to harass Megan, and she'd raced to her friend's rescue, arriving in the parking lot of the sheriff's office disheveled and furious, with her face flushed and her red hair standing out around her head like a tumbleweed.

And there had stood Dallas—cool, cocky, and so handsome that Beth Ann had practically lost her breath. He was tall, dark complected, with dark brown hair, a square chin, and cold, blue eyes that had appeared to warm a degree when Beth Ann jumped out of her clunker of a car. Considering that he was dressed in a custom-made suit that probably cost more than Beth Ann's clothes budget for the entire decade, merely made her more determined to stand up to him.

And shc'd donc just that, both then and the next time they'd met when Beth Ann had spilled the bowl of flour she'd been using to coat chicken for frying, and Dallas had referred to her as a "red-headed snow lady." The fact that he went speechless half an hour later when she'd returned to the room cleaned up and wearing one of Megan's designer dresses had gone a long way toward soothing her initial chagrin.

But now, once again, Dallas had arrived on the scene when she looked less than her best.

She ignored an urge to drop back to the floor behind the counter and pretend she wasn't in the store. Instead she forced a welcoming smile. "Hey Dallas. Guess your being in Barbourville means it's your turn to check on Megan and the triplets."

Dallas grimaced. "You'd guess right. However, I'm sure Megan must be sick of her uncles dropping in to check on her and the girls, so I haven't worked up the courage to stop by her house yet. Considering that you're her best friend, I'm hoping you'll let me buy your lunch while I ask your advice about something."

"Okay." Beth Ann struggled to keep her tone matter-of-fact. She figured Dallas knew how attracted she was to him, but she also knew it was an attraction that had no future. Dallas was a sophisticated, educated, and successful attorney from Chicago. She was a single mom from a small town who had a huge debt hanging over her head. Not exactly the girl of every man's dreams.

Or *any* man's dreams, for that matter.

But she found she couldn't control the direction of her own dreams when Dallas walked up to the counter and looked directly into her eyes. His lips, as usual, curved upward just slightly, as though he found the world to be an amusing place with him on the outside looking in.

He rested his elbows on the counter and leaned forward. His fragrance, a subtle blend of crisp aftershave and expensive soap, wafted across the counter and slammed into Beth Ann's senses. Darn, but the man smelled good.

He lifted his brows. "Is Sonny's Diner okay with you, or are you sick of eating next door to your shop?"

Beth Ann glanced down at his hand lying outstretched on the counter. His fingers were long and slender and his nails were neatly trimmed. She wondered if they were manicured. She curled her own fingers into her hand. She really had no excuse to keep biting her nails now that she knew Trevor was going to be all right. She moistened her lips. "I'm not tired of the diner, but there's a new place a couple of blocks from here named Jill's Soup Bowl. I'm trying to throw some business her way. Would you mind going there?"

"Any place is fine with me. Can you close the shop long enough to eat?"

"Sure. Just let me go wash my hands. I've been unpacking my winter merchandise today."

"Isn't the first of September a little early to get winter fashions in?"

"Not really. Of course, I won't put them out for a while, not until early next month, but it's best to get everything in as soon as possible so

I'll be ready when the time comes. I've been working all morning and I'm more than ready for a break. I'll be right back."

She walked quickly to the small bathroom tucked in the back of her shop and looked in the mirror above the vanity. Just as she had feared. There was a streak of dirt on her right cheek, and her hair was as unruly as usual. She splashed a bit of water on her face, dragged a brush through her hair, and touched her lips with a rosy gloss that didn't clash too badly with her hair. She then squared her shoulders and stepped back out front.

Dallas had moved over to the front window and stood staring into the street. He turned when she stepped into the room and shot her that wicked grin that always set her heart to fluttering. "That didn't take long. My car's out front if you want to ride."

"I'd rather walk if you don't mind."

"That's fine with me. I've been driving all morning and could stand to stretch my legs."

Beth Ann paused to flip the sign in her door from OPEN to CLOSED before preceding Dallas into the street. Half a dozen people called a greeting to her while she pulled out her keys and locked the door, and she responded with a nod and a smile. Most everyone was headed to Sonny's Diner next door. It was the most popular restaurant in town, so she was doubly glad she and Dallas wouldn't be eating there. She looked forward to having a little time alone with him.

Not that she *should* be looking forward to it. She *should* be running away, not falling into step beside him, but she was tired of always doing what she should. Today she wanted to enjoy herself, even if it was only for an hour. And even if she was going to feel lonelier than ever when he went away again.

Foot traffic thinned as they made their way down the street. The day was heating up as the sun moved overhead, and Dallas paused long enough to slip his sport coat off and fold it over his arm.

He wore a navy, short-sleeved polo under the sport coat, and Beth Ann couldn't help but notice the breadth of his shoulders and the way his dark hair barely brushed the collar of his shirt. He noted her stare and shot her a grin, which she pointedly ignored.

"We turn left here at Moser Avenue, and the restaurant is just down the block," she said. "The food's excellent, if you like soup and sandwiches or a salad."

Dallas nodded. "Sounds good to me. Mostly I'm interested in something cold to drink. The day's hotter than I expected. Isn't Barbourville's temperature supposed to be cooler because of the altitude?"

"We're some cooler, sure, but it's still summer, you know. It's not supposed to be cold yet. Just wait until January rolls around."

"Try January in Chicago if you want cold weather."

"No thanks. Cold weather isn't my cup of tea. And speaking of tea, let me recommend Jill's orange iced tea. It tastes good any time of year."

"You talked me into it. And here we are it seems." He stopped in front of a structure that had once been a downtown residence. The wide front porch, painted a cool white, sported half a dozen tables topped with green tablecloths and small pots of red geraniums. A wooden sign on an easel beside the front door pictured a soup bowl, with the restaurant's name written in script across the top of the board.

"Let's eat inside if you don't mind," Beth Ann said. "It's probably cooler." She didn't mention that it would definitely be more private, and she wanted Dallas all to herself for a half hour or so.

Five minutes later a young waitress had seated them at a table in the front room, which had no doubt served as a parlor when the house was new. Only one other couple shared the room, and they were seated on the far side of the dining area.

Beth Ann and Dallas placed their orders for orange tea and looked over the menu until the waitress returned with their drinks and a basket of homemade bread.

Beth Ann looked up at the waitress. "A Caesar salad and vegetable soup for me."

"Make mine a club sandwich and a bowl of red beans and rice soup." Dallas closed his menu, reached for Beth Ann's, and handed both to the waitress.

"The bread is excellent here." Beth Ann picked up the basket and selected a muffin. "I'm famished. Would you like a roll or a muffin?"

"A muffin sounds good." Dallas reached for the basket and his fingers brushed against Beth Ann's. She closed her eyes for the briefest of seconds. What fun it would be to pretend they were a couple, that this was a date, and that Dallas had come to see her for reasons that had nothing to do with asking her advice about his beloved niece.

But make believe was a luxury she couldn't afford. She drew her hand back and grabbed her glass of iced tea. "You wanted to ask my advice about something?"

"First, tell me about Trevor. How's he doing?"

Beth Ann bit her lip. Even now, when she knew her son would eventually recover from the injuries he'd suffered at the hands of a hit-

and-run driver, she didn't find it easy to talk about his accident. She cleared her throat, took a deep breath, and forced a smile. "Trevor's doing much better. His arm is still in a sling, but he got off of the crutches two weeks ago. He was thrilled about that."

"I don't blame him. And has Daniel made any progress toward catching the driver who hit him?"

Beth Ann blew her breath out and shook her head. "I'm afraid not, but then he didn't have much to go on. Trevor was riding his bike out on highway one-fifty-two headed to his friend Jimmy's house when he was hit. No one saw the accident happen, and Trevor couldn't tell us anything because the car came up behind him and knocked him and his bicycle into the ditch. Thank God old Mrs. Gallaher came chugging along a few minutes later and saw him lying there. She stopped to check on him, realized how badly he was hurt, and flagged down Sean Smith who had a cell phone and could call for help."

Dallas shook his head. "It doesn't sound as though there was much Daniel could do."

Beth Ann shrugged. "He tried, that's for sure. He went over Trevor's wrecked bike with a fine-toothed comb and found some red paint that had to have come from the vehicle that struck the bike. Then he called on several other sheriffs in this part of the state, but none of them had seen any suspicious vehicles with front-end damage. They finally concluded it must have been a drug runner. The sheriff in Wayne County has been having a lot of trouble with people heading north on the interstate with carloads of cocaine they pick up in Miami."

"But the interstate doesn't run through McCray County, so why would a drug runner be over here?"

"Daniel thinks some of them may come this way to avoid the extra surveillance in Wayne County. If that's the case, and it really was a drug runner, they'll never locate the car that hit Trevor."

Beth Ann reached into the bread basket, grabbed a roll, and started crumbling it into her bread plate, which still held half of her muffin. When she realized what she was doing, she stifled a sigh. Clearly her nerves were getting the best of her, a common occurrence when she talked about Trevor's accident. She immediately laid the remnants of the roll on her plate and dropped her hands into her lap.

Frowning, she looked up into Dallas' eyes, which had darkened with sympathy, and spoke again without thinking. "It's bad enough, knowing that the person who practically killed my son may never be apprehended, but . . ." She paused, sorry she'd let Dallas' obvious concern steer her down this path. She bit her lower lip, wishing she could think of a quick change of subject. Some of her problems she simply couldn't bring herself to talk about, not to Dallas or to anyone else.

A frown touched Dallas' brow and his eyes narrowed. Clearly he wondered why she'd stopped talking mid-sentence. Thankfully, Beth Ann saw the waitress approaching with their food. She looked up and forced a bright smile. "Enough chatter from me. I really do hope you like the food here. Most people in town who have tried it enjoy it."

Dallas' frown deepened. He glanced at Beth Ann, then toward the approaching waitress, and obviously decided that now was not the time to pursue their conversation. He lifted one shoulder in a half-shrug, then remained silent while the waitress set the food in front of them, asked if they needed anything else, and then left left them to their meal.

Beth Ann took a sip of her soup and watched as Dallas tasted his.

"Excellent!" he said, and then all was quiet for a few minutes while they devoted their attention to their food.

By the time they finished eating, the other couple had paid for their meal and left, so Beth Ann and Dallas had the dining room to themselves.

Beth Ann laid her napkin beside her plate and looked across the table. "So what's this advice you're looking for, Dallas? Wait. Let me guess. You want to know if Megan will run screaming into the street when she discovers that another one of her uncles has shown up in town. Right?"

Dallas grimaced. "Something like that. Only worse."

Beth Ann grinned. "At the risk of sounding rude, what could be worse?"

"Being told that I want to stay in town for the next few weeks."

Chapter Two

Beth Ann choked on a sip of iced tea and coughed for several seconds before she could breathe normally again.

Dallas' expression was one of chagrin. "Are the thoughts of my being around for a while that bad?"

"No, no, you just surprised me, that's all. Why on earth are you planning to stay for a few weeks? You have a career and a life in Chicago if memory serves me correctly."

"You're right, I do. But of the three of us in the firm, I have the lightest workload at the moment, so Dayton and Denver felt I should be the one to come."

"But why? I know you and your brothers

promised Megan's mom on her deathbed that you would watch over Megan, but I have to tell you, Dallas, Megan is getting a little tired of you three acting as though she's not got enough sense to live her own life, especially now that she's married and has started her own family."

Dallas flinched. "You don't pull any punches, do you?"

Beth Ann sighed. She didn't want to hurt anyone's feelings, but Megan was her best friend and as such deserved first place in her loyalties. She looked into Dallas' eyes and shook her head. "It doesn't make sense, Dallas, you dropping everything and moving down here to watch over Megan. You've got to be able to see that."

Dallas shrugged lightly. "Oh, I see it, Beth Ann. And I assure you, I'm not here because I want to be. It's because of Dayton."

"Dayton? What do you mean?"

Dallas shrugged again. "I've never really tried to explain this to anyone before. The thing is, even though Dayton and Denver and I are triplets, we are different in lots of ways. Dayton was born first, by just a few minutes, but he's always seen himself as the elder brother. He's the most serious and he takes everything to heart more than either Denver or I do."

Beth Ann didn't really see where Dallas was

going with this, but she nodded. "Okay," she said by way of encouragement.

Dallas continued. "As you know, we were much younger than Megan's mom, and we adored our older sister. Sometime after she married and then had Megan, her energy level dropped and she seemed tired all the time. Everyone assumed she just wasn't getting enough rest. When the doctors finally found the cancer, they did everything they could to save her, but it was too late. She died when Megan was five."

"And Megan told me that you boys were only ten," Beth Ann commented. "That's an impressionable age. Losing your older sister like that must have been very difficult."

"It wasn't easy on any of us, but I think it affected Dayton the most. He simply took things to heart more than Denver or me. The thing is—and I know this isn't logical—but I think Dayton somehow worries that Megan's fate will mirror her mother's."

Beth Ann frowned, truly puzzled. "What on earth do you mean?"

"I think Dayton is afraid, now that Megan is married and has given birth, that she may become sick, just like our sister did. He feels an obsessive need to watch over her. He couldn't be here himself because he has a big court case coming up soon, so he asked me to come. Frankly, I wanted to refuse, but I knew it would eat him up inside, worrying about Megan. I know it doesn't make any sense . . ." He paused, then shrugged.

Beth Ann felt the beginnings of a headache nipping at her forehead. "You're right, Dallas. None of this makes any sense. But obsessions rarely do. I'm sorry for Dayton, but I'm sorrier for Megan. She deserves an opportunity to get on with her life."

"You're right. I know you're right. So you think I should just turn around and go home?"

"I didn't say that." A thought had suddenly occurred to Beth Ann, one that caused her headache to begin to fade.

Dallas leaned forward. "What do you mean? Is there some way I can actually be of help to Megan?"

"To be honest with you, Dallas, I'm not sure Megan really needs any help, but I believe Daniel would welcome you with open arms."

Dallas sat back and shook his head. "You must be kidding, Beth Ann. Daniel's a nice fellow, but having his wife's uncles hanging around all the time can't be any fun for him."

"No offense, Dallas, but Daniel's used to interfering uncles. He's had enough of his own to contend with, so I don't think he really resents you and your brothers."

"Maybe not, but that doesn't mean he'd welcome me living in his house for a while."

"He might. The thing is, with Daniel being the sheriff, he's on call most of the time, and when he has to go out on a call at night, he worries about leaving Megan alone with the three babies. If you were staying in the house, he could count on you to help out if she needed someone."

"You really think so?"

"I know so. Daniel's mentioned his concerns to me half a dozen times. I've assured him that I could dash across the street and help Megan any time during the night that she needed me, but he still worries."

"If you're right, then I'd better talk to Daniel before Megan even knows I'm in town."

"Definitely. He may be at the station right now if you want to swing by there."

A dazzling smile brightened Dallas' face. "You've been a tremendous help, Beth Ann. Thanks so much."

"You're welcome." Beth Ann pushed her chair back from the table. "I'd better get back to the shop."

Dallas reached across the table and placed a

hand over hers. "Before we leave, I want to ask you something else."

Beth Ann swallowed swiftly. Dallas' hand resting on top of hers scattered her thoughts, and while she loved the sensations his warmth created, she couldn't allow herself to become distracted.

Not when he appeared so serious.

She used the need to scoot her chair back up to the table as an excuse to move her hand. Then she moistened her lips. "Ask me what?"

He left his hand lying on the table near her, as though inviting her to reconnect with him. "Just before our food arrived, you mentioned something about the hit-and-run driver who hurt Trevor, but you never finished your sentence. What were you about to say?"

Beth Ann felt a blush brightening her face, the bane of being a redhead, unfortunately. She made it a rule not to talk about her troubles, especially to someone like Dallas who had never had money worries, but something about the expression of interest in his eyes made her decide to confide in him.

"I was merely going to say that if we had caught the driver, I might have gotten some money out of his insurance company to help with Trevor's expenses. As it turned out, all the medical costs fell to me, and I don't have health insurance."

"Ah, I see." Dallas cocked his head to one side and regarded Beth Ann with a slight frown. "Are you in debt pretty deep?"

"I'm afraid so. As you can imagine, Daniel and Megan have tried to loan me money, but I don't borrow money from friends, especially when there's a good chance I can't pay them back."

"I can respect that. But what about family members? Don't you have anyone who could help you out in some way?"

Beth Ann sighed. "Trevor and I are pretty much by ourselves. His dad's people all moved to Oregon within a couple of years after Jim died. They still send birthday and Christmas gifts to Trevor, but they wouldn't have the resources to help with medical expenses. And as for my family, my father's been dead for years and my mother passed away shortly after Trevor was born."

Dallas' brows lowered. "So you didn't have anyone at all after your husband died?"

"I had my great aunt Brenda. Trevor and I lived with her until she died. She willed me her house, you know. She's been gone for six years now, and I still miss her."

Dallas grimaced. "I can't imagine not having

family around. So I guess what all of this means is that you need to figure out a way to earn more money by yourself."

"Right. And believe me, I've tried. But the dress shop just doesn't turn a big profit, no matter how many hours I put in."

"What about your house?"

"What about it?"

"As I recall from the one time I was there, it's huge. Maybe you could turn it into a bed and breakfast."

Beth Ann shook her head. "Thanks for trying, Dallas, but that's out of the question. The house is always in need of repairs, and I can't afford them, let alone the cost of meeting codes for a bed and breakfast."

"Have you looked into it?"

"No, because that would be a waste of time. I simply can't deal with anything else right now anyway. Which reminds me, I'd better get back to the shop. I sure won't make any money with that CLOSED sign up."

Dallas pulled out his billfold and placed a twenty on the small tray holding their ticket. From the slight frown touching his brow, Beth Ann figured he was still thinking about her problems, and she already regretted mentioning them. She didn't want anyone feeling sorry for her, especially not Dallas Vance.

She jumped to her feet. "Ready?" she asked, then turned without waiting for an answer and hurried toward the door, leaving Dallas to trail her.

Dallas escorted Beth Ann back to her shop, thanked her for her help, got back into his car, and headed out to the sheriff's office. With any luck, he'd find his nephew-in-law and get Daniel's permission to spend some time at his house helping out with the babies.

Truth be told, he'd rather be headed back to Chicago, but then he'd just spend all of his time worrying about Dayton, who would be worrying about Megan. Denver was the most laid back of the three, but even he was apt to fret about whether Megan was managing to cope with three babies at once. Strange, Dallas mused, how triplets ran in the family. First him and his two brothers, now Megan's three girls.

But it was wonderful too. He couldn't have been happier when Daniel called to tell them the news. He and Dayton and Denver had all made arrangements for other attorneys to cover their cases long enough for them to fly to Tennessee and see Megan and the babies.

And the girls were darling, of course. They took after their mother with that dark chestnut hair, but they had their father's topaz eyes. Dallas had taken one look at them and fallen in love, as had his brothers.

But their own mother had often mentioned how difficult it had been for her to deal with three babies who generally were all hungry or all wet or all colicky at the same time. And as Dayton had recently pointed out, their mother had a full-time nanny and a part-time nurse-maid to help her.

Megan had no one except her husband, who was often away at work, and occasionally her neighbors and friends.

So here he was, making his way toward the rather dull concrete block building that comprised the sheriff's office and the county jail. He hoped Beth Ann had been right and that Daniel wasn't going to view his presence as interference.

He pushed open the door and stepped inside. Daniel looked up from the papers on his desk and rose with a welcoming smile. "Dallas! Good to see you. Were we expecting you?"

Dallas grimaced. "Actually, no. I slipped into town and shanghaied Beth Ann for a bite of lunch and some advice. I hope she isn't wrong in what she told me."

"Which was?"

Dallas took a deep breath and exhaled quickly. "That you wouldn't mind me hanging around town for the next few weeks to help you and Megan with the babies."

Daniel's brows shot up. "A few weeks?" He stepped around his desk and walked to Dallas' side. "I have to ask, Dallas. What experience do you have with babies?"

"None at all. How about you?"

"Well, none, but . . . hmmm. I see what you mean. But still . . . look, Dallas, I admire you and your brothers' determination to live up to the promise you made your sister when she was dying, but—"

Dallas threw up a hand. "I know what you're going to say, Daniel, and it's not that we don't trust you and Megan to handle your own lives, but it's hard for us to break an old habit. Besides, Beth Ann thought you might welcome someone staying in the house at night in case you have to answer a call."

Daniel nodded slowly. "She's got a point about the nights. Days are pretty well covered, fortunately. With this being the first set of triplets born in Barbourville, everybody wants to pitch in and help. My Aunt Evelyn and my mother are there about every day, and the church ladies bring food at least once a day and sometimes twice, but I do hate to leave Megan alone at night to try to deal with three babies.

Invariably, if one starts crying, the other two join in. You realize, though, that Megan may not see this the same way we do."

"You can convince her if you tell her that my presence will ease your mind."

"I guess. And it wouldn't be a lie. Your being there would sure make me feel better if I had to answer a call at night."

"That settles it then. How long before I can come by the house?"

"We'll both go right now. I'd as soon go ahead and get Megan's agreement so you can get settled in."

Two hours later, Dallas had successfully placated Megan, which fortunately hadn't been as much trouble as he'd expected. For an uncomfortable moment, he'd suspected she had an ulterior motive for agreeing to his suggestion so readily, but she'd immediately distracted him by leading him over to three lace-draped bassinets sitting side by side in the parlor. He'd spent a good twenty minutes cooing over his three beautiful great nieces, but then Daniel's Aunt Evelyn had arrived to sit with them, so he'd greeted her and then excused himself to go out to his car and retrieve his luggage.

Megan had disappeared, so Dallas let himself back into the house and carried his suitcases up the stairs and into one of the guest bedrooms in Daniel's and Megan's large Victorian house. For reasons he preferred not to examine too closely, he made a beeline for one of the rooms on the front of the house, a room that looked out on Redbud Road and directly across the street toward Beth Ann's house, another large Victorian.

The most noticeable difference between Daniel's house and Beth Ann's was that hers showed definite signs of neglect. The white paint was peeling, the roof shingles looked thin, and the yard was badly overgrown. Even one of the faded green shutters dangled on only one hinge.

But it had potential. Dallas was no expert, but he could certainly judge that the house would be a beauty if it was properly maintained. And it would surely be more profitable than Beth Ann's clothing store. This part of the state drew a large number of tourists who came for the cool mountain air during the summer months and the flamboyant leaf colors during the fall.

He shrugged. No sense in thinking along those lines. Beth Ann had already said no. And he couldn't blame her for not wanting to take on more responsibility. She was a widow with a son to raise, a large debt hanging over her head, and a house that must eat money on a daily basis.

Nope, the lady didn't need any more troubles, which meant Dallas had better keep his distance. No sense letting something get started between them when the road ahead would be both rocky and much too short.

He turned away from the window and walked out into the hall. The smell of coffee wafted up from the kitchen, and the mingling of various voices from below suggested several of Daniel's relatives had stopped by, probably with covered dishes to leave for supper. Dallas knew from previous visits in Barbourville that Daniel's relatives were extremely good cooks. He smiled and followed his nose down the stairs.

Dallas' first night of nanny duty was blessedly uneventful. Apparently Daniel got no calls. At least Dallas never heard the phone ring, and if the triplets cried, he didn't hear that either. In fact, he slept so soundly he felt downright guilty when he awoke at seven the next morning. Hoping he hadn't shirked his duties on his first night on the job, he pulled on his jeans and stuck his head out into the hall. The nursery was only three rooms away, so he eased down the hallway in his bare feet and peeked inside. The triplets' cribs were empty.

Next he walked to the head of the stairs and

stood quietly, listening for sounds from below. After a few seconds, he detected Megan's voice, then Daniel's. Figuring he had a few minutes before he would be needed, Dallas went back to his room, grabbed some fresh clothes, and hurried to the guest bathroom down the hall.

Twenty minutes later he had showered, shaved, and dressed for the day in jeans, a T-shirt, and his most comfortable walking shoes. He didn't know quite what to expect, but hey, he figured he could face whatever was in store for him.

His optimism was a bit premature, as he discovered some five minutes later. By the time he got downstairs and stepped into the kitchen, Daniel had left for work and in his place were his mother, his Aunt Evelyn, and two ladies Dallas had never met before. Turned out they were volunteers from Megan's church who had signed up to help out from 7:30 until noon. When they left at noon, two other volunteers would take their place.

And Daniel's mom and aunt were extra hands in case the volunteers weren't enough. Anyway he counted it, he came up with three babies and five ladies, including Megan, to take care of them.

Suddenly, Dallas felt about as useful as the proverbial fifth wheel.

But Miss Evelyn, who had just laid a sleeping baby in one of the three bassinets lined up against the kitchen wall, greeted him with a cheerful "Good Morning" and insisted he have a seat at the kitchen table while she scrambled some eggs. She appeared delighted to be preparing him a real Southern breakfast complete with ham, grits, and biscuits, and Dallas didn't have the heart to tell her he would have preferred toast and black coffee.

Twenty minutes later, after turning down seconds for the fifth time, Dallas managed to escape into the backyard. Megan, obviously, didn't require his services at the moment, and what he needed was a few minutes by himself and a chore that would help him work off some of those breakfast calories.

He looked around the backyard for something to do. Everything was neat as a pin. The flowerbeds were weeded, the grass was freshly mowed, and even the hedge was neatly trimmed. Maybe he'd better just go for a run.

He let himself out through the gate in the picket fence and walked up the driveway to the street, then paused to stare at Beth Ann's house.

It looked even worse than it had from his upstairs window the afternoon before. A flagstone path leading from the sidewalk up to her front porch needed weeding badly. The front porch could use a coat of paint, and the wooden steps leading up to the porch looked considerably less than sturdy.

But the house itself was a beauty, and Dallas could easily envision it freshly painted, with, say, a soft yellow paint and white trim like the B&B he'd visited in Birmingham a couple of years ago.

Beth Ann's yard could use some serious work too, but it sported huge oaks and spreading maples that could offer shade for a few group-ings of outdoor furniture. City folks would pay dearly to stay in such an appealing place.

Dallas needed some way to work off his breakfast, and he had just had an idea. If he wasn't mistaken, Daniel's Uncle Josh, the attor-ney, and his Uncle Richard, the architect, had offices just a few blocks away. It couldn't hurt to walk down and see if they had time to talk to him. Between the two, he should be able to find out what would be involved in turning Beth Ann's house into a bed and breakfast.

Chapter Three

Beth Ann had decided to walk to work that morning instead of driving so she could save money on gas. After all, she needed to save every penny she could manage. Trevor's medical bills loomed over her head like a mountain about to fall on her, and she couldn't envision getting out of debt for the next twenty-five years or so.

And there was still Trevor's college to think about. He wanted to be a doctor, or so he thought now, and Beth Ann was determined to help him meet that goal. Which meant she should be saving money, but that was impossible when some months she couldn't even pay all of her bills.

But this morning was bright and crisp, with

an unexpected promise of fall in the air, and she soon found her steps quickening and a smile easing onto her face. It was hard to stay sad when the air smelled of dew and dry leaves and sausage patties frying at Sonny's.

She nodded to half a dozen people as she passed them on their way to partake of that first cup of coffee at the diner. Soon she arrived at her own shop, where she unlocked the door and stepped inside.

Despite hard times, Beth Ann always experienced a quick lift of her spirits when she stepped over that threshold each morning. Her shop smelled of new clothes and of apple-scented potpourri, which she kept in small dishes scattered around the store.

She flipped the light switch and glanced around to make sure she hadn't overlooked anything the evening before when she closed up. She tried always to keep the clothes correctly arranged by sizes and by styles.

She didn't sell expensive clothes, nor did she sell cheap imports. She tried to stick with middle-of-the-line merchandise that the women of McCray County could afford. Although increasingly, it seemed, local women were going either to Smithwood to shop at the large discount store there, or, if they wanted upper-end clothing, to Knoxville or to Atlanta.

Which accounted for her slow sales, but Beth Ann didn't really know what she could do about it. And she didn't know how to do anything but sell clothes. She had never wanted to go to college really, because she had never wanted to be anything except Jim Stanfield's wife, and that was what she had become the week after they'd graduated from high school.

She and Jim had been young and deeply in love and frightfully happy. She hadn't understood then that life could throw curves at you. Sharp and biting curves that swept you down into deep holes you thought you could never climb out of again. She'd felt that way when Jim died in a car accident barely six months after they were married, but she'd had a baby on the way and she'd had no choice but to go on living for the child's sake.

And then Trevor was born and she had a compelling reason to go on living.

And she would continue to go on, both for Trevor's sake and because that's just what people did.

She finished her quick perusal of the store and stepped to the back room to start a pot of coffee. She'd work on the books some this morning and then finish inventorying the new merchandise.

She was on her second cup of coffee and her

third box of merchandise when the bell above her door jingled. She looked up, then gulped so quickly she almost strangled. My gosh! She'd never seen Dallas so casually dressed before. His jeans had faded to a soft blue, which contrasted nicely with his darker blue T-shirt. He needed a cap, she decided, then changed her mind. That head of dark hair was entirely too attractive to hide under a cap.

She set her coffee cup on the counter and stepped around to greet him. "Good morning! Have the McCray triplets already run you off?"

He grinned. "The triplets were the least of my worries this morning. Between Daniel's relatives and Megan's church ladies, I was decidedly outnumbered and definitely unneeded."

Beth Ann laughed. "I suspect you'll find that to be true every morning. What about last night?"

"All quiet on the home front. Which is good, I guess. I really need a little practice on how to take care of babies before I'm thrown into the fray."

"Good luck on that! I've barely been able to get my hands on one of them, and I live right across the street. Seems everybody in town wants to help take care of the babies because they're the town's first set of triplets. How about you and your brothers? Did you get tremendous amounts of attention because you were triplets?"

"Pretty much. We eventually got tired of it and insisted on trying to be individuals. We dressed differently. We went to different colleges. We even tried to develop individual personalities."

"And yet today you're all together in a law practice in Chicago," Beth Ann observed.

"Yes. The ties are stronger than we had realized, but sometimes I think . . ."

"What?"

"Oh, nothing. Listen, can you take a break and let me buy you a cup of coffee at the diner? I have news I'd like to share with you."

"I'd love to join you, Dallas, but I've got a mess on my hands this morning. I've been opening boxes of merchandise, and half of it's wrong or of inferior quality. I'll have to send it back to the supplier, but first I need to finish going through the boxes. I wouldn't mind a break, though. I've got a pot of coffee in the back room. I'll be glad to pour you a cup and you can share your news with me right here."

"Fine! I take mine black."

Beth Ann cleared off a small table where she usually displayed costume jewelry, then asked Dallas to pull up a couple of chairs while she went after the coffee. She was glad she kept extra mugs in the back, even if she did have to serve Dallas coffee in one announcing the seventy-fifth anniversary of the McCray County Bank.

Once they were settled down in the chairs, coffee cups in hand, she looked at him with raised brows. "Okay, what's the big news? Are the triplets talking already?"

Dallas frowned. "I don't think so. Babies don't start talking when they're a month old, do they?"

Beth Ann struggled so hard to suppress a laugh that she felt her face growing warm. She shook her head, but Dallas had already caught on.

"You were pulling my leg. Babies don't do much of anything at one month old, do they?"

"Actually, they do quite a bit, but walking and talking aren't on the list. Forgive me, Dallas. I was being facetious and didn't realize you were so, ah—"

"So ignorant about babies?"

"I was going to say something more polite, but just now I can't think what that would be." She grinned. "Anyway, what's your news?"

Dallas set his mug on the table. His eyes sparkled with anticipation. "I've been talking with Josh and Richard McCray this morning."

"Okay." Beth Ann stared at him, waiting for him to continue.

"In their professional capacities."

"Okay. But why did you want to talk to an attorney and an architect? What's going on?"

"I talked to Josh first. He tells me that your house is already in a commercial district, so there would be no zoning problems, and Richard assures me that structurally your house is likely to be sound. Also, he thinks it could be brought up to code with only a few thousand dollars worth of changes."

"For a bed and breakfast, you mean?"

"Of course! Your house would be perfect, Beth Ann. I know the summer months are gone, but if we hurried, we could take advantage of the folks who crowd into town to see the fall foliage."

Beth Ann closed her eyes and shook her head slowly. "I thought you understood, Dallas, that I can't afford to do the work on my house that would be required to turn it into a bed and breakfast."

"Well, of course I understood. I was thinking I could be an investor—"

Beth Ann slammed her coffee cup onto the table and jumped to her feet. She turned and glared down at Dallas. "I see. The rich knight rides into town and tosses a few thousand dollars at the poor maiden, who is supposed to accept with abject gratitude and turn her life over to him. Well get real, Dallas. I'm not taking your money, and I'm not turning my house into a bed and breakfast."

Dallas opened his mouth as though to speak, but Beth Ann didn't slow down. "I have an injured child to care for and a business I can barely keep afloat. When am I going to find time to run a bed and breakfast? And before you say you'd help, remember that you'll be going back to Chicago in a few weeks. Who's going to help then, Dallas? I'd be alone with a monstrosity of a bed and breakfast I couldn't keep up. Now please stop this nonsense."

By the time she finished her rant, Beth Ann realized that the color had drained from Dallas' face. He got to his feet slowly, then sighed.

Beth Ann's fury was suddenly supplanted by regret. She took a half-step backward. "I'm sorry, Dallas. I shouldn't have—"

He tossed a hand up to stop her. "Don't apologize, Beth Ann. You're right. You tried to tell me and I didn't listen. I'm more sorry than I can say that I've added to your problems. I'll not bother you again."

Beth Ann watched him walk to the door. He turned back and smiled, a bit wanly. "Thanks for the coffee. I'm sorry I upset you." Then he let himself out of the door and closed it softly behind him.

Beth Ann stood perfectly still for several seconds while the realization dawned on her that she had once again allowed her temper to get the better of her. She had shouted at poor Dallas, who had merely been trying to help her.

He would probably tell Daniel and Megan how she had behaved, and while they would always remain her friends, they would be disappointed in her.

And Dallas would probably never speak to her again.

She dragged feet that felt like blocks of concrete over to the front door, flipped the sign over to CLOSED, and walked into the back room where she promptly burst into tears.

Chapter Four

Dallas wished he could kick himself all the way back to Megan's. Since that wasn't possible, he settled for mentally chastising himself with every step.

How could he have been so stupid? So insensitive? He knew how proud Beth Ann was, and still he'd barged in with his offer to finance a project she had absolutely no interest in tackling. No wonder she'd yelled at him. It was no more than he deserved.

And now they wouldn't be comfortable around each other anymore. They wouldn't joke with each other. They wouldn't flirt.

Damn, but he'd made a mess of things.

He needed to talk to Megan. She and Beth

Ann were best friends. Maybe Megan could suggest how he might be able to make it up to Beth Ann.

But when he got to the house, Daniel's Aunt Evelyn informed him that Megan was upstairs feeding the babies. He decided to make himself scarce for a while.

He walked downtown, browsed in the drugstore until he found a paperback novel he knew would hold his interest, then wandered back to Megan's.

The second shift of church ladies had shown up by that time, bringing with them several covered dishes supplied by other church ladies, and they insisted Dallas eat with them. Megan joined them, but the babies were fussy and she seemed preoccupied so he didn't want to bother her with his problems.

After lunch, he offered to help with the dishes, but when the ladies insisted they would take care of everything, he decided to take his book into the backyard and settle down in a lawn chair under a maple for a quiet read.

It was a pleasant afternoon, warm but not hot, and he had just become engrossed in his book when a distant SPLAT . . . SPLAT . . . SPLAT . . . SPLAT drew his attention. He laid his book in his lap and listened.

SPLAT . . . SPLAT . . . SPLAT . . . SPLAT.

There was a regularity to the sound that reminded Dallas of stories he'd heard about Chinese water torture.

SPLAT . . . SPLAT . . . SPLAT . . . SPLAT.

Within seconds he knew he couldn't stand it any longer. He had to find the source of that unbelievably irritating noise.

He stood, laid his book on the lawn chair, and followed the sounds.

He took a few steps toward the front of the house, paused, and listened.

There it was again.

He pushed open the gate leading from the fenced backyard to the driveway and the street.

The sounds grew louder.

He stopped at the curb and looked around. He couldn't see any source for the noise, but it sounded as though it was coming from Beth Ann's yard.

Without pausing to think, Dallas hurried across Redbud Road. He stopped at the end of Beth Ann's driveway, noting that her dilapidated Chevrolet was parked near a pathway leading to the front porch. Of course that didn't mean she was at home. As close as her shop was, she could have easily walked to work.

The noise sounded again, apparently coming from Beth Ann's side yard. Maybe someone was trying to break into her house.

Moving more quietly now, Dallas cut across the lawn and eased around the corner.

Trevor stood a few feet back from the side of the house. His left arm was in a sling but that didn't stop him from using his right arm to throw a ball against the house where it hit with a loud splat. Trevor would catch the ball when it bounced back his way and then throw it again. Dallas thought he had never seen a little boy look more lonely.

He stepped around the corner. "Hey, Trevor, whatcha doing?"

Trevor looked up quickly. His eyes brightened and a smile lit his face. "Hi, Mr. Vance. I heard you were in town. How are you?"

Dallas smiled back although his initial reaction to Trevor's gaunt face and uneasy stance was one of dismay. Obviously Trevor had suffered a great deal since his accident. Where the boy had once been a carefree child, his eyes now reflected a degree of maturity that was unusual for a twelve-year-old. Getting blasted by a hit-and-run driver during a simple bike ride must do that to a boy. Dallas forced a grin. "I'm doing fine, thanks. You look as though you're doing okay yourself."

"Yeah. I'm off crutches now, and in three more weeks I'll be out of this sling. Are you helping Miss Megan out with the babies?"

"Theoretically. In actuality I'm just hanging around her house being bored. Want to throw some with me?" He nodded toward the ball in Trevor's hand.

"Sure. After that maybe you could help me start the mower. I think I can push it with one hand, but I can't seem to get it started."

"Okay, although I'd love to take that chore off your hands. The way Megan's church people are feeding me, I need all the exercise I can get. Maybe I can do the mowing, and you can pull some of those weeds that are growing in the cracks of the flagstone path."

"That'd be neat. Mom was planning on doing the mowing and the weeding when she gets home this afternoon, but the days are getting shorter and she doesn't have much daylight left after she closes the store. I'd like to be able to help her out some."

"Sounds good to me. How about we do the chores first and then, if there's any daylight left, we can throw the ball some?"

"Okay. The mower's over there in the tool shed. It's gassed up and I checked the oil, but it still won't start for me."

"I'll see what I can do." Dallas spoke with more confidence than he felt. It wasn't that he'd never pushed a mower before. He'd grown up in the suburbs and had mowed his share of grass, but it had been a few years. Besides, Denver had been the mechanically minded of the three brothers, and it had been his responsibility to keep the mower tuned.

Fortunately, Beth Ann's mower needed only a little extra priming before it started. The motor coughed a few times but soon caught and started running smoothly despite the near-deafening racket it made. Trevor pointed to the front yard and Dallas nodded his understanding. The front yard needed attention pretty badly so he would start there.

By the time Dallas had finished both the front and the side yards, the afternoon was waning, and he decided he'd better put the mower away and make tracks across the street. He didn't want Beth Ann to find him working in her yard. He wouldn't be able to fault her if she jumped to unfavorable conclusions about his motives.

But he'd promised Trevor to throw with him, and Trevor deserved a little recreation. The kid had pulled weeds with his right hand for a good portion of the afternoon. He'd completely cleared the flagstone path and then started on one of the overgrown flowerbeds beside the front porch steps.

So as soon as the mower was put away and the tool shed door closed, Dallas turned to

Trevor. "Where's that ball we were going to throw?"

Trevor rolled his right shoulder. "If you don't mind, Mr. Vance, I'd just as soon put that off until tomorrow. My arm's a little sore right now."

"Having to do everything with one arm must get a little tiring."

"Yeah, it does. But if you're not busy tomorrow, I'd sure like to take you up on that offer."

"I won't know for sure until tomorrow, but unless Megan's church people go on strike, I figure I'll be free."

Trevor giggled, sounding more like a little boy than he had all afternoon. "The church people won't go on strike, believe me. So I guess I'll see you tomorrow."

"I suspect so. Rest that arm tonight, buddy."

"I sure will, Mr. Vance. Bye now."

Dallas threw up a hand in farewell and headed across the street. Daniel's car was in the driveway, along with a couple of others he didn't recognize. He suspected Daniel's extended family members had brought supper, and he had worked up quite an appetite, so he hurried into the house.

He soon discovered that he'd guessed right about the company and the food. Both were enjoyable, and by 10:30 when he went up to his bedroom and looked out the window, Beth Ann's house was completely dark.

By noon the next day, Dallas had finished his paperback and was contemplating walking back to town for another. He hadn't seen any signs of Trevor being out and about yet, and he certainly didn't intend on calling the boy. He remembered very well how much young people liked to sleep the morning away, and he had a feeling Trevor needed the rest to help him heal.

Dallas begged out of eating lunch at Megan's, explaining that he was still stuffed from the breakfast Aunt Evelyn had insisted on feeding him, so he grabbed his billfold and headed down Daniel's front walk.

"Hey, Mr. Vance. Where you going?" Trevor stood on the sidewalk across the street, ball in hand.

Dallas stopped and threw up his hand in greeting. "I didn't know you were out and about yet. I'm on my way to the drugstore to buy a book, but that can wait. Do you want to throw some now?"

"I'd rather walk to town with you, if you don't mind. Mom's still a little scared of me going far by myself, and all my friends are away at camp this week. I couldn't go to camp this year."

"Sure, you can come along with me." Dallas wondered if Trevor couldn't go to camp because of his injuries or because his mother couldn't afford whatever fees might be involved. Of course he couldn't ask. Instead he said, "Have you had lunch yet?"

"Nah. Mom left me a sandwich in the refrigerator, but I wasn't hungry."

Dallas figured a cold sandwich wasn't that appetizing anyway. "I haven't eaten either. How about we walk to your mom's shop and see if she'll join us for a burger?"

"That'd be great!"

"Let's go then." Dallas waited for Trevor to join him and they stepped off together toward downtown. He wondered if Beth Ann would still be furious with him. If she was, he'd just have to apologize again and hope this time she would forgive him.

Beth Ann had struggled all morning to keep from crying, and she had succeeded, but just barely. She couldn't believe she'd been so rude to Dallas yesterday. He'd only been trying to help her, after all.

And she suspected that he'd helped Trevor work in her yard yesterday afternoon. She hadn't even realized until this morning that work had been done in her yard. After all, it had been dark when she got home from the shop last night, and Trevor hadn't said a word about having done any work outside. Of course, he'd been engrossed in a rerun of *The X-Files* and naturally wouldn't have thought to mention anything so commonplace as yard work.

She'd have to try to get home early enough this evening to walk across the street to Megan's house and thank Dallas for his help. She would be embarrassed, knowing she'd screamed at him like a banshee and he in turn had mowed her lawn for her.

But maybe someone else had done it? She'd better call home and ask Trevor to be on the safe side. She didn't want Dallas to think she was making up excuses to see him.

She wasn't, was she?

My gosh! How much more high school could she get? She wasn't eighteen any more, and Dallas wasn't captain of the McCray County High football team. He was a sophisticated, highly eligible bachelor from Chicago. He might be attracted to her, but that's where it would have to end. She had a child to raise and he had a life to return to.

And she was not going to give into tears now. Not after getting through the morning without crying. Having no customers to wait on had given her plenty of time to think, which hadn't helped matters any.

But she had made it. And now it was

lunchtime. She'd just get her sandwich and a soda out of the mini fridge in the back and . . .

The bell over the front door jingled. She looked up. A customer at last.

But it wasn't a customer. Dallas pushed the door fully open and stepped back. Beth Ann felt her heart jump into her throat, then sink rapidly toward her heels. Why wasn't he coming on in?

Oh wait. He was holding the door open for someone. Trevor?

"Hi, Mom." Her son hurried into the store. He smiled widely, the first time she had seen him so happy in days.

"Guess what, Mom? Mr. Vance wants to take us to lunch. Could we go, please? I'd really love a burger from the diner. Could we?"

Beth Ann forced her gaze up and looked directly into Dallas' eyes, which were sparkling merrily but which also held a hint of, could it be nervousness? She gulped. "Ah, well, I don't . . . ah . . ."

Dear heavens? Could she be any more inarticulate? She moistened her lips and tried again. "Well, I'm not sure—"

Dallas tossed up a hand to stop her. "I don't blame you for hesitating, but what if I apologize again and then promise not to harass you anymore about opening a B and B? Would you go then?"

Beth Ann felt blood rushing to her face. "Really, Dallas, I'm the one who should be making promises not to misbehave. I'm so—"

"Hey, Mom. Sorry to interrupt, but all the booths in the diner will be full soon. Could I run on ahead and get us a seat and place our order?"

Beth Ann tore her gaze away from Dallas and glanced down at her son. She had been neglecting him lately, even though she'd felt as though she had no choice. Her creditors didn't care that she had a young boy at home alone.

So she couldn't bring herself to say no, even though she hadn't planned to let Dallas spend any more money on her. She forced a smile. "Sure, sweetheart. Tell Sonny that Dallas and I will be there as soon as I lock up the store. And order the daily special for me, whatever it may be."

"I'll take a burger," Dallas said, reaching to ruffle Trevor's hair. "Thanks for going ahead and getting us a seat, buddy."

"No problem!" Trevor grinned and made a dash for the front door.

With nothing left to serve as an excuse, Beth Ann forced herself to look at Dallas. His frown was slight, but his eyes reflected an emotion that appeared to be concern.

"Have I totally messed up our friendship?" he asked.

"You?" Beth Ann stared at him with

widened eyes. "You just tried to be helpful. I was terrible to you. And on top of that, I suspect you were kind enough to mow my grass yesterday afternoon."

"Only part of it. I'm hoping you'll give me permission to finish it this afternoon. I need the exercise."

"Look, I know my yard's a mess, and I appreciate you wanting to help out, but . . ."

"I mean it, Beth Ann. I really need the exercise. I go to the gym most days in Chicago, plus I don't eat biscuits and gravy every morning for breakfast. Come to think of it, I *never* eat biscuits and gravy in Chicago. So I sure would appreciate the opportunity to work in your yard. I'd work in Daniel's yard but it's already perfect."

"Well, that's true. Mikie Smith takes care of Daniel's yard and you wouldn't want to knock him out of the opportunity anyway. He needs the money."

"That's settled then. I'll work in your yard for the exercise. Now, we'd better get on over to Sonny's or Trevor will be wondering what happened to us."

Beth Ann felt a smile tugging at her lips. "You're sure making a good impression on Trevor."

Dallas grinned. "He's a great kid. You've done a wonderful job with him."

Beth Ann blinked rapidly, aware that Dallas couldn't have said anything that would have pleased her more. She cleared her throat. "Thanks, Dallas. And thanks for all you're doing for him. Now let me grab my purse so we can get on over to the diner before my perfect son consumes your burger."

Dallas laughed, a cheerful sound that chased away the last of Beth Ann's blues.

Chapter Five

Beth Ann was not surprised that lunch with Dallas and Trevor turned out to be a highlight of her week. Even though Sonny's prices were reasonable, she hadn't allowed herself to eat there in a while, and she now found herself reveling in the camaraderie of the customers, the mouth-watering fragrances wafting from Sonny's kitchen, and the pure pleasure of relaxing in agreeable company while she ate.

Trevor also clearly enjoyed the occasion. From the admiring glances he sent Dallas' way, Beth Ann realized that her son had found himself a role model. She'd always known he needed a man in his life, and Daniel McCray had been a great friend to her and Trevor until lately, when his new family consumed all of his extra time. She was pleased that Dallas was befriending Trevor, even though it might only be for a few weeks.

The idea of Dallas' leaving threatened to derail Beth Ann's good mood, so she pushed the thoughts away and made it a point to enjoy the remainder of her lunch. When they'd finished and it was time for her to go back to work, she felt much more comfortable about Trevor, knowing that Dallas would be walking back home with him.

Soon after she reopened the store, a storm blew in, followed by a sharp drop in temperatures. This taste of fall sent customers flocking to Beth Ann's store looking for long-sleeved shirts and lightweight jackets. She was suddenly immersed in sales, so she didn't get a chance to call home until long after her normal five o'clock closing hour.

Trevor answered with a hurried "Hi," then said that he'd been invited across the street to have supper with the McCrays. He explained that Dallas had called him to say that Megan had more food on hand than a pro football team could polish off and that Trevor's appetite was urgently required. "I can go, can't I, Mom?"

Beth Ann gave her permission and tried not to feel sorry for herself when she closed her shop and went home to a dark house. She was too exhausted to cook just for herself, so she settled for a bowl of cereal, then stepped outside to gaze across the street.

Daniel's and Megan's house was filled with light. Half a dozen cars lined Redbud Road, and the sounds of conversation and laughter drifted across the street whenever someone opened a door to enter the house or to leave.

Beth Ann knew she would be welcome if she wanted to join them, but she didn't feel like crossing the street and warming herself at Megan's hearth. She was too tired to be decent company tonight. She would wait up for Trevor and then turn in for the evening.

She wasn't proud of the single self-pitying tear that wound its way down her cheek, but she wouldn't lie to herself. Most of the reason she wouldn't cross the street tonight was because Dallas was there, and she was simply too exhausted to cope with the deluge of emotions he engendered in her.

She was finding it more and more difficult to hide her attraction to Dallas, and she didn't want to embarrass herself by letting her emotions show in front of all the people gathered across the street. The last thing she needed was to give folks another reason to pity her.

And they *would* pity her because they would

understand the same as she did that any sort of relationship between her and Dallas Vance was doomed from the beginning. That anything more than a flirtation would be as ephemeral as the fireflies that flickered and faded away when summer gave way to fall.

Sighing, she cast one last lingering look across the street, then squared her shoulders and went back inside her house.

The next morning dawned clear and, as Beth Ann had expected, the brief cool spell was over and the day had turned as warm as early June. Since Trevor had been out later than usual the night before, she left him sleeping and walked to work. The townspeople were already outside working. Yards were getting mowed, which served not only to even out the grass but also to mulch the first of the autumn leaves that had been downed by yesterday's storm.

The shop was practically dead after the previous day's rush, so she straightened the racks and then brought her books up to date. When noon approached, she tried to call Trevor but got no answer.

Suddenly too restless to spend another minute by herself, she grabbed her purse, taped a GONE TO LUNCH sign in the window, and set out for home. The sunlight immediately cheered her, and she was especially glad she had decided to play hooky when she turned onto Redbud Road and saw Dallas crossing the street toward her house. A plastic grocery bag hung from his right arm, and he gripped a heaped-up tray in his hands.

"What's going on?" she called.

"Come give me a hand," he called back.

Beth Ann met him when he stepped onto the sidewalk and relieved him of a foil-covered paper platter that was about to slide off the top of the tray.

"What's all of this?" she asked.

Dallas continued walking toward her house and she was forced to fall into step beside him. "I'm just helping Megan and Daniel," he said. "There was a terrible mixup at their house this morning."

"Oh no! What happened?"

"Two different Sunday school classes thought that today was their day to supply lunch, so around eleven-thirty, five cars pulled up and people unloaded so much food, Megan had no place to put it all. I relieved her of some roast beef, fried chicken, macaroni and cheese, green beans, some sort of congealed salad, homemade yeast rolls, and, oh yes, pecan pie and German chocolate cake."

"You're kidding!"

"What do you think I have on all of these paper platters? I'm sure glad you're here to help me and Trevor put it away."

Beth Ann hurried ahead to open the door leading into her kitchen. "I'm glad too. This beats a cold sandwich any day. Where's Trevor?"

"He'll be along in a minute. When I left Megan's headed this way, she was loading him down with a quart of gravy and a bowl of creamed potatoes."

"Wonderful! I'll just clear off the dining room table and set out some plates."

"Sounds good to me. I'm starved. Miss Evelyn had a hair appointment this morning and didn't stop by until too late to fix my usual Paul Bunyan breakfast."

Beth Ann turned to look at him. "What kind of breakfast?"

"You know, the kind a giant needs when he's a lumberjack and plans to cut down an entire forest before lunch rolls around."

Beth Ann grinned. "Well, we'll try to make up for your lack of a substantial breakfast. Is that Trevor I hear at the door?"

Dallas set the tray on the kitchen counter. "He's probably got his one good arm full and can't open the door. I'll take care of him while you get the plates out."

Forty-five minutes later, the three of them were happily complaining of being stuffed.

"I'll never eat again," Trevor declared, right before he forked up his last bite of pecan pie.

"That's sure going to cut down on the grocery bills around here." Beth Ann winked at Dallas.

Dallas grinned. "Somehow, I suspect that *never* is going to be rather short-lived."

Beth Ann clasped a hand to her heart. "Don't tell me that. I was already planning on all I could buy with the extra money."

Trevor laughed, then pushed himself to his feet. "I'm going to run the empty gravy jar and the mashed potato bowl back across the street if that's okay, Mom."

"We have to wash them first."

"Me and Mr. Vance did that while you were setting the table."

"Okay, run along then. And be sure to thank Megan for sharing with us."

"I will." Trevor dashed toward the kitchen. The sound of the kitchen door slamming announced his departure.

"He's a great kid," Dallas said.

"Thanks! I think so. I appreciate your spending so much time with him."

"I appreciate *him* spending so much time with me. The days would get boring for me otherwise. I'm glad it dried up today so I can get the mower out again."

"It's sure a help to me, you mowing the lawn."

"Don't mention it. But I do need you to come to the backyard with me and show me something."

"Okay. Just let me put the leftovers in the fridge and stick the dishes in the dishwasher."

"Need any help?"

"No thanks. You go on and I'll catch up."

Beth Ann watched Dallas turn and go out the back door. What could he want her to show him? She quickly stored the leftovers and shoved the dishes into the dishwasher. Then she stepped onto the porch and slipped her feet out of her good shoes and into the work shoes she liked to keep handy. A few seconds later she found herself wading through grass that was much taller than she had realized.

Dallas watched her approach with a broad grin. "Stepping high, I see."

Beth Ann felt heat rushing to her cheeks. This was downright embarrassing. Then she looked into his twinkling eyes and grinned back at him. "Hey! No smart aleck remarks from the hired help, please."

Dallas swung his arm up and gave her a crisp salute. "Yes, ma'am."

"That's better. I expect proper respect around

here." She stepped to his side. "What did you want me to show you?"

"Where your property line is. I figured your neighbor to the back here might not want me mowing his yard."

Beth Ann frowned. "What neighbor? I don't have a neighbor except on either side, and there are fences on the property lines there."

"No, I mean that neighbor." Dallas pointed to a small house half hidden among shrubs and mature trees. The house faced away from Beth Ann's, fronting on the street running parallel to Redbud Road.

"Oh that! That's not a neighbor. That's on my property."

"You own that house too?" Dallas frowned. "I don't understand."

Beth Ann cocked her head to one side. "What's not to understand? It's part of my property. It belongs to me. Not that it's of any benefit to me. I pay taxes on it, but I can't rent it. It would need too many repairs."

"Did you inherit it along with your house?"

"Yes. My great grandparents built both houses at the same time. The smaller one—we always called it the cottage—was for the care-taker and his wife, who was the housekeeper. They lived there until they died, and then it sat empty until my great aunt Brenda inherited the property. She rented the house up until a few years before she died. By the time I inherited it, it needed new plumbing, wiring, and a whole lot more. I had a new roof put on it, but that's about all I could afford. But I do try to keep the yard mowed."

"Could I see it?"

"You want to see the cottage?"

"Could I? I know you need to get back to the shop, but I would enjoy seeing the inside. My father used to do some woodworking, and I've always enjoyed looking at older places."

"Well, sure. Come on. I keep a key hidden on the front porch."

Ten minutes later, Dallas was running his hand over the intricate carving that surrounded the mantle in the cottage's living room. "Walnut, I think," he murmured. Then, more loudly, "Could you hold the candle a little higher?"

Beth Ann took a step closer to him. "Really, I don't mind going back to the house and getting a flashlight." She had explained when they stepped inside the house that she kept the electricity off and the plumbing drained so the house would require as little maintenance as possible.

"Thanks, but I refuse to put you to any more trouble. You need to get back to the shop but . . ." Dallas reached for the candle, then stepped across to the double doorway leading into the dining room. "Whoa! Would you look at the door facings? I can't believe the amount of work that's gone into these."

Beth Ann squinted at the dark wood, then shrugged. "Mr. Potter probably did those. The cottage was designed for him and Mrs. Potter so he helped with the construction, or so I've been told. I always heard he was a good carpenter."

"Good? He was more than good. He must have loved the craft if he did the work in this place."

Beth Ann looked around her. The flickering light from the candle did little to illuminate the room. "I never paid much attention to tell you the truth."

Dallas smiled. "I would be surprised if you had. We all tend to take for granted the things that we grew up with."

He stretched his arm out as though to hand Beth Ann the candle, then pulled it back and merely stared at her for several seconds.

"What?" Beth Ann ran a hand over the top of her head. "Do I have cobwebs in my hair?"

Dallas continued to stare. "Sorry, but your hair is the most amazing color when the candlelight hits it. I've never seen anything quite like it."

Beth Ann dropped her hand to her side and moistened her lips. "You haven't?"

"God, no. There's this underlying glitter, almost like spun gold with an overcoat of—I don't know what to call that shade of red, but I know I like it."

"You do?" Beth Ann pulled a deep breath in, then exhaled slowly. "I really am capable of stringing more than two words together. You just sort of, ah, I don't know exactly."

Very slowly Dallas lifted a hand and gently brushed a strand of hair back from her forehead. "Does it occur to you that neither of us seems to be finding the words to express what we're feeling?"

Beth Ann nodded, then frowned. "What are you doing?"

"Looking for some place to put this candle because I'm going to kiss you. Or at least try to." He set the candle on an end table. "What do you say about that?"

Beth Ann knew she was playing with fire, but occasionally flames were just too tempting to resist. "I say," she murmured, stepping closer, "that sometimes actions definitely speak louder than words."

A twinkle brightened Dallas' eyes. "So you're saying that since words are failing us, we should try actions instead?"

"Something like that." Beth Ann looked up into his face and watched the twinkle in his eyes change to a spark of desire. He slowly wrapped his arms around her, carefully pulled her toward him, and lowered his lips toward hers.

The kiss was everything Beth Ann had ever imagined and a great deal more. Her senses were immediately enveloped in essences of Dallas, the warmth of his body, the gentleness of his lips, the enticing fragrance of his cologne. He was perfect for her in every way. He wasn't too tall, so she didn't need to stretch to reach his lips. Nor was he so broad that when she wrapped her arms around him, she felt diminished by his size.

He pulled her closer, deepening the kiss, and Beth Ann felt her blood speeding up, swirling through her veins and spinning her thoughts into a thousand fragmented pieces. Nothing, she was convinced, could pull her out of the delicious trance that Dallas was weaving.

"Mom?"

Except the sound of Trevor's voice, of course. She reluctantly placed her hands on Dallas' shoulders and pushed.

He ended the kiss and pulled back a half inch. "What?"

"Trevor's calling me."

Dallas paused and listened.

The voice from outside came again. "Mom?"

Dallas sighed, then slowly released her. With

a half-smile and a twinkle in his eyes, he murmured, "Children are such annoying little creatures. Why do people want them anyway?"

"Seems like I had a reason once upon a time but I can't remember now what it was." She reached to touch her lips, as though she could capture the kiss with her fingertips, then hurriedly picked up the candle and headed for the door. "I'd better let him know where we are. Ready?"

"Yeah, let's go. But I need to talk to you as soon as we get a chance."

Startled by his serious tone, Beth Ann stopped and turned to look at him, but he merely stepped around her and went on out to the porch where he paused to call to Trevor. "We're over here, Trev. Come on back."

Trevor trotted up a few seconds later. "Hey there, Mr. Vance. Whatcha doing?"

"I was merely admiring the cottage. Your mom tells me we need to mow all the way to the street back there."

"This house is called Potter Place," Trevor informed him. "It's named after Mr. and Mrs. Potter who used to live in the cottage."

"Thanks! Well, I'd better get busy if I'm going to get the grass cut before dark."

"I'll go open the tool shed and pull the

mower out." Trevor turned and hurried toward the side yard.

Beth Ann stepped up beside Dallas and grabbed his arm. "Don't get the idea that you're going to mow the afternoon away while I spend the whole time wondering what you want to talk about. What is it?"

Dallas reached to grasp her hand, then held on to it while he turned to face her. "I don't want you to think that what I'm about to ask you is anything but a direct question. There's no ulterior motive here, Beth Ann. You need to understand that up front. I'm not trying to butt into your business and I'm not looking for ways to provide help you don't want."

Beth Ann's mouth turned dry. He was so serious, almost angry it seemed. "Whatever, Dallas. Just don't keep me in suspense. What is it?"

He took a deep breath. "I want you to sell me the cottage and whatever of its contents you're willing to part with. I know it's been in your family for a while, but it's obvious you don't love that house the way I would. If you will consider selling it, I would insist on a full appraisal before we decided on a price so I wouldn't accidentally cheat you. Will you think about it?"

"You're serious, aren't you?"

"Absolutely!"

"But what would you do with it?"

"First of all, I'd restore it. And before you tell me I don't know what I'd be getting into, let me assure you that I do. My parents raised me and my brothers in a huge house in the suburbs, and my father loved nothing better than puttering around the house on weekends. He considered himself a handyman of sorts, and I got a kick out of helping him. Denver was mechanically inclined, and Dayton was a bookworm, but I liked fiddling with the plumbing and wiring and sometimes helping Dad with his woodworking."

"But what would you do with it once you had it restored?"

"I'd hang onto it, if that's what you're wondering about. Since Dayton and Denver and I will probably be making numerous trips to visit Megan and our great nieces, we might want to stay in the cottage rather than piling in on Daniel and Megan every trip. I might rent it on occasion, too, if you wouldn't object to having renters in your backyard."

"Oh, that wouldn't be a problem since you can barely see the cottage from the house. So sure, I'll think about it, Dallas. In the meanwhile, I'd better get back to the shop."

"Right." He released her hand. "See you later this afternoon."

"Okay. See you." Beth Ann headed to the house to change shoes before going back to the shop. She had a lot to think about this afternoon. The possibility of having Dallas Vance living in her backyard was both tempting and terrifying at the same time.

And, she admitted to herself, it was terrifying simply because it was so tempting. Which probably meant she should turn him down flat. But resisting temptation had never been one of her strong suits.

So what to do, what to do? She shook her head. Darned if she knew how to answer that question.

She heard the mower sputter and then catch, its loud growl spreading across the lawn and scattering her thoughts. She shrugged and turned to wave to Trevor and Dallas before heading back to the shop.

Chapter Six

Beth Ann decided before breakfast the next morning that she was going to sell the cottage to Dallas.

She knew the dangers. In fact, she'd thought of little else all afternoon yesterday and well into the night, and she'd discovered that this particular temptation was one she simply couldn't resist. The thought of having Dallas Vance occasionally living in her backyard was just too appealing to ignore.

And the money would be a boon too. She had no idea how much to expect, but she didn't think it could be less than fifty thousand dollars for the cottage and its furnishings combined, which would go a long way toward paying off Trevor's medical bills.

She could hardly wait to tell Dallas, but the sun was barely up, and there were no lights on in Megan's house across the street.

She would come home for lunch again today, Beth Ann decided, and if Dallas wasn't working in her yard or visiting with Trevor, she'd look him up and give him the news. She hoped he'd still be interested in buying now that she'd made up her mind to sell.

She brewed some coffee and settled down at the table in the kitchen to look over the morning's paper while she waited for Trevor to wake up. She liked to be sure he had a decent breakfast before she left for work in the mornings, but she didn't want to wake him for another hour or so.

Half an hour later, someone knocked on the back door. Beth Ann glanced at the clock and frowned. People didn't come calling in Barbourville at half past six in the morning unless something was wrong.

She tossed the newspaper onto the table and hurried to the door where she pulled the curtain aside and looked out. Dallas stood outside. When he saw Beth Ann looking through the glass, he smiled and held up a brown paper bag.

Beth Ann unlocked the door and opened it. "What's wrong?"

"I saw your light on and hoped you were up. How about some breakfast?"

"So nothing's wrong?"

"I'm pretty darn hungry. Does that count?"

"Not for much, no." But she smiled before she stepped back and motioned him in. "What's in the bag?"

"Bagels. But not just any bagels. Denver sent me a care package."

"Your brother sent you bagels from Chicago?"

"Yep."

"Why? You could get bagels in the grocery store here."

"Those are imitation bagels. These are the real thing. Do you have any coffee?"

"Yes, but . . . do you know what time it is?"

"Is it too early? Should I leave and come back later?"

Beth Ann shrugged. "This is a little weird, that's all. Is everything okay at Megan's and Daniel's?"

"Great. Or so Megan informed me when I got out of bed to find out why three babies were screaming at the tops of their little but very powerful lungs. Megan soon got them settled down, but I was wide awake by that time. Then

I saw your kitchen light on and decided to share my bagels with you. You should feel honored."

Beth Ann couldn't help but wish she'd slapped on a little makeup this morning before she came downstairs. Thank goodness she'd pulled on jeans and a sweatshirt instead of wearing just her gown and robe. She nodded toward the table. "Sit down and make yourself at home. I'll get you some coffee."

"Great. I'll be setting the bagels and cream cheese out."

A few seconds later, Beth Ann returned with a steaming cup of coffee and a couple of table knives. "What else do we need?"

"Not a thing if you don't mind eating off of a napkin." He had spread two paper napkins out and placed a bagel on each. "Do you like bagels?"

"Sure." Beth Ann scooted Dallas' coffee across the table and seated herself. "I'm glad you came over."

"Because you love bagels?"

She took a bite of her bagel and chewed a minute. "Mmmm. This is good."

"I told you. Is that why you're glad I came over?"

"Not entirely. I wanted to tell you that I'll sell the cottage to you if you're still interested in buying."

Dallas laid his bagel down and stared at her. "You're serious?"

"Absolutely. Are you still interested?"

"Sure am." He grinned. "This is great. I'll want to get someone lined up to do an appraisal as soon as possible. Do you know anybody?"

"No, but Daniel could probably tell you who to see."

"I'll check into it this morning. See you later." He got up, walked around the table, and bent to surprise Beth Ann with a quick but torrid kiss. Then he straightened, grinned, and hurried across the kitchen to the back door. He disappeared without looking back.

Beth Ann touched her lips, which tingled from the lightning bolt of electricity that had leaped to life when Dallas kissed her. Yep, selling the cottage to him was definitely a dangerous move. She grinned and jumped to her feet, more eager to face the day than she had felt in a very long time.

Beth Ann had been in her shop for less than an hour when Dallas stopped by, a wide grin on his face.

"I've already lined up an appraiser," he said. "Daniel sent me to his Uncle Richard, who recommended a man he uses in his architecture business. I called Mr. Warren and he agreed to look over the cottage tomorrow. Do you think you can get the electricity turned back on today?"

Beth Ann reached for the phone. "I think so. One of my customers works for the power company and she might be able to pull some strings."

Five minutes later she placed the receiver back in its cradle and nodded. "It will be taken care of this afternoon before three."

"Great! Now I've got to round up an antique dealer or two."

"Antique dealers? What on earth for?"

"To check out the furniture, of course. Or do you not want to let the furniture go with the cottage?"

"Well sure, you can have the furniture. But it's just old furniture. I don't think antique dealers would want to bother with looking at it."

"I'd prefer to get it appraised anyway. Otherwise, I wouldn't feel right about keeping it, and it fits the cottage so well, I'd hate to lose out on it."

"Okay, if that's what you want. But, really, I'd intended to let it go with the cottage."

Dallas shook his head. "You'd be cheating yourself if you did, and I don't intend to let that happen. I'm prepared to pay whatever price the appraisers set, but if you prefer to have your own people look at it, that's fine with me."

Beth Ann struggled to keep from frowning. Dallas' comment about her cheating herself had rankled a bit. Did he not think she was an astute businesswoman? She lifted her chin. "I don't need my own appraisers. I already have a price in mind that I wouldn't consider going below."

"Great! I assure you we'll go with whichever is higher, your price or the appraisal. I really want that cottage." He grinned. "Not much of a bargainer, am I?"

Beth Ann felt a smile tugging at the corners of her formerly grim lips. Darn the man. He knew exactly how to charm her. "Go away, Dallas Vance. I have work to do, and so do you."

"You're absolutely right. I've already spotted a couple of nice looking antique stores. I'm going to go talk to the owners now. See you later."

Beth Ann leaned against the counter after Dallas hurried away. His enthusiasm was hard to fathom, but it was also infectious. Having the little cottage repaired and restored would be good for the neighborhood. Not to mention the fact that having it off her hands would be a load off her mind. And she could certainly use that fifty thousand dollars she intended to insist on.

Over the next few days, Beth Ann saw very little of Dallas. He dashed in and out of the store occasionally, first to thank her for getting the electricity turned on so quickly, then to ask how much of the property she was willing to let go with the cottage.

Fortunately, she could answer that question easily. She remembered that Mr. Potter had planted a row of lilacs that visually separated the two yards, so she suggested that the boundary line be established on the north side of the lilac bushes.

Dallas had nodded. "Exactly what I was thinking. I've got the name of a surveyor. I'll call him and ask him to shoot the lines and draw up some new plot maps so I can get those filed for us."

"Sounds like a plan to me," Beth Ann said in a tone she hoped gave the impression that she knew what in the dickens he was talking about.

"I'm glad you agree. I'll bring the plot maps in for your approval when they're finished."

"Okay." Beth Ann smiled weakly. "Fine."

"See you later."

The next time Beth Ann saw Dallas was near the end of the business day on Friday. He stopped by the shop to get her approval on the new property lines and also to tell her that he'd managed to get all of the appraisals done. His eyes danced with enthusiasm when he asked Beth Ann if she would be free to meet with him that afternoon to discuss price. Because, he explained with a devastating smile, the sooner the sale was finalized, the sooner he could get to work on the cottage.

Beth Ann was more than ready to discuss price. She'd begun to feel guilty about the amount of time Dallas had invested in this project. What if he wasn't willing to meet her price of fifty thousand dollars? Would she be willing to take less? She didn't think so, but she'd feel really awful turning Dallas down now.

The bell above the door jingled. Beth Ann looked around and saw that Mrs. Ford and her daughter had just entered the shop. They were two of her best customers, and she needed to wait on them.

She turned back toward Dallas and lowered her voice. "Why don't you plan on having supper with Trevor and me? I always grill hamburgers on Friday afternoons, and I'd be happy to fix an extra one for you. You could come by around seven and we'll talk price then."

"Sounds good to me. What can I bring?"

"Maybe some chips if you don't mind. I think Trevor's polished off all of ours."

"I'll pick some up. See you at seven."

At closing time, Beth Ann rushed home, changed into her jeans and a cotton blouse, and mixed up her great aunt Brenda's recipe for hamburger patties, which was one of Beth

Ann's favorites. After shaping six good-sized portions, she arranged them on a platter and shoved it into the refrigerator before grabbing the matches and a bag of charcoal briquettes and heading outside.

Dallas was already in the side yard spreading a plastic cloth over the picnic table. Five plastic grocery bags rested on a lawn chair.

He had obviously showered because his hair was still a bit damp, and he had changed into a bright red tee. He looked toward her and smiled just a bit sheepishly. "I hope you don't mind that I came over early. I forgot to ask you what kind of chips you and Trevor like, so I got five different kinds, and I also brought some cookies and a couple of cans of baked beans."

"Trevor will be thrilled, I assure you."

"Where is Trev, anyway?"

"He's inside getting the silverware together. He'll be out in a second."

"In that case, could we talk price now? I'm really anxious to find out if you're going to accept my offer, which is based on appraisals for the cottage and the furniture and the land. If you're satisfied with my offer, I can get started with the renovations right away. If you're not, well, I'll have to see if I can meet your price."

Beth Ann lowered herself into a nearby lawn chair. Was she willing to take less than fifty thousand dollars? She honestly didn't know. She gulped. "Okay, what is your offer?"

"Remember, Beth Ann, this is based on the appraisals, but if you're not satisfied, we'll talk further. My offer—and as you know, this is negotiable—my offer is one-hundred-and-forty-five thousand dollars."

Beth Ann was certainly thankful she was already sitting down. She would have hated for Dallas to realize how affected she was by the mention of that much money. Dear heavens, she couldn't expect to earn a hundred-and-forty-five thousand dollars if the shop turned a healthy profit for the next ten years.

Not that she was going to accept his offer, of course. She was not that naive. Obviously Dallas thought of her as a charity case, and he was hoping to ease her financial burdens by drastically inflating his offer.

She pulled a deep breath into her lungs. She hadn't accepted charity when Trevor's daddy was killed. She hadn't accepted charity when Trevor was born. She hadn't accepted charity when Trevor had been injured so badly by that hit-and-run driver.

And she certainly wasn't going to accept charity from Dallas Vance.

She placed the palms of her hands on the arms of the lawn chair and very purposely pushed herself to her feet. She moistened her lips, swallowed, and lifted her chin.

"Thank you for your very kind offer, Mr. Vance. But you can take your one-hundred-and-forty-five thousand dollars and go straight to hell."

Chapter Seven

Looking back on that afternoon, Beth Ann wondered if she really would have had the nerve to turn her back on Dallas and stalk away after hearing his offer for the cottage. That had certainly been her intention when she got to her feet.

However, she had barely put one foot in front of the other when Dallas rushed to her side, planted his hands on her shoulders, and stared directly into her eyes. He blew his breath out in a long sigh and shook his head.

"Darn it, Beth Ann, if you're not the prickliest human being I've ever met. What on earth have I done to make you so mad at me?"

Beth Ann felt heat moving up her neck and

onto her chin. Soon, she knew, her entire face would be a shade darker than her hair. She stepped away from Dallas' grasp and turned her back to him.

He moved to stand in front of her.

She stared at his shoes.

He stepped closer. "I mean it, Beth Ann. I want to know what I've done to upset you. I told you all along that I would raise my offer to meet your price. What *is* your price anyway?"

Beth Ann could scarcely speak around the lump that had set up shop in her throat. When she finally managed to force out an answer, her voice was barely above a whisper. "Fifty thousand."

"A hundred and fifty thousand, did you say? No problem. That's just barely above the high range of the appraisals, so I'll be happy to meet your price."

Beth Ann cleared her throat but didn't look up. "I said fifty thousand."

"You said *what*?"

Beth Ann jerked her head up and glared at him. "Fifty. I said fifty thousand dollars. Have you gone deaf as well as batty?"

"My God!" Dallas met her gaze, then threw his hands up. "You thought I was patronizing you, didn't you? Don't you realize that I know better than to pull a stunt like that? You insult me, Beth Ann. You should know that I think too highly of you to be condescending toward you. The only reason I didn't show you the appraisals was because I knew you'd insist on the low end, but even the low end was a hundred-and-thirty-two thousand."

Beth Ann plopped her hands onto her hips. "Then somebody's jerking you around, Dallas. The cottage and its furnishings couldn't possibly be worth that kind of money. In Chicago, maybe, but not in Barbourville, Tennessee."

"That's where you're wrong, my girl. People love cottages these days—particularly older cottages—and folks are willing to pay a bundle for them. And the furniture is handmade for the most part. On top of that, some of it is hand-carved by Mr. Potter, I feel sure. He has a very distinctive style. I could take the bedroom suite alone to Chicago and sell it for fifty thousand dollars."

"Are you serious?"

"Do I look like I'm kidding?"

Suddenly Beth Ann felt an urge to grin, but taking into account the fury that crackled in Dallas' eyes, she decided grinning wasn't a good idea at that particular moment. She ducked her head to hide her emotions.

"Look Dallas, I'm sorry. I'm really, really sorry for misjudging you and for telling you where to go and for—"

"Hey, Mom. Could somebody give me a hand here?"

Both turned toward Trevor's voice. He stood at the top of the porch steps with an armful of dishes and a fistful of silverware. Rarely had she been so glad to see her son, who was unknowingly providing her with an excuse to escape Dallas' questioning. "I'll be right there sweetheart," she called.

"Oh never mind, I'll go." Dallas' tone was less than gracious, and the quick glare he tossed in Beth Ann's direction before he turned away clearly imparted his opinion that they had unfinished business, but Beth Ann pretended not to see. She figured Dallas would cool off soon, and she was too delighted at the thought of all that money to stay irritated with him.

She cupped her hands at each side of her mouth and yelled toward Dallas' back, "By the way, I accept your offer."

"I'm really lucky that the summer is behind us and construction workers have some free time now," Dallas informed Beth Ann very early on Wednesday morning nearly three weeks later. He had been cutting across her lawn on his way to the cottage when she'd seen him and invited him into the kitchen for a cup of coffee.

She placed a mug in front of him on the table,

then sat down across from him. "You're especially lucky that you could talk Richard Mc-Cray into serving as both your architect and contractor. I hear he's hard to get."

"I can see why. He's good. Did I tell you that he has redesigned the entrance by enclosing the front porch in order to brighten up the living room?"

"No, but that sounds like a vast improvement."

"I think it will be." He glanced at his watch. "The carpenters should be here within the next half-hour, so I'd better go. But first, tell me how Trev is doing."

"Frankly, I don't think he's floated back to earth yet. This is the first school year I've been able to buy him the kind of school supplies and clothes he wants. And he's relieved to have his arm out of that sling. So all in all, he's very happy. I still can't believe all of this myself. It sure feels good to have my debts paid and a nice nest egg put away."

Dallas grinned and reached across the table to grasp her hand. "You have no idea how much fun I'm having with this cottage, Beth Ann. I really can't thank you enough for selling it to me."

Beth Ann glanced down at his hand and took a quick breath. She and Dallas had dropped their flirtatious behavior and seemingly settled into a quiet friendship, but she still couldn't suppress the attraction she felt for him. She longed so deeply to lift his hand and press it against her cheek. But she didn't have that right. Instead she smiled and stood, gently pulling her hand from his grasp. "I need to get Trevor up so he can get ready for school."

Dallas stood also. "And I need to have the cottage unlocked when the carpenters arrive. Thanks for the coffee. See you later."

"Later," Beth Ann echoed while Dallas let himself out the door. She sighed and shook her head. "Don't you dare complain," she murmured to herself while setting their mugs in the sink. "You knew what kind of heartache you were letting yourself in for when you sold to him."

She stepped to the window and looked out at Dallas' departing back, then grinned. "But considering how he looks in those tight-fittin' jeans, it's all gonna be worth it."

Before noon that day, Beth Ann had decided to close her shop and go home for lunch. If she timed her arrival just right, the workmen would be breaking for their noon meal and maybe she could talk Dallas into joining her for a sandwich.

She walked from the shop to her house in near record time, then suppressed a sigh when she saw the man who was standing on her flagstone walk. She had no choice but to call out a friendly greeting.

"Hello, there, Judge McCray."

The judge was still a handsome man for his age. He tipped his hat, exposing a head of thick, white hair. "Hello, Ms. Stanfield. How are you these days?"

"Fine, thanks, Judge. Have you been across the street visiting your great nieces?"

The judge's blue-green eyes sparkled. "Prettiest babies I ever saw. And have you noticed that they've got the McCray eyes?"

"I certainly have. Even Megan is thrilled about that. She says Daniel's eyes were the first thing that attracted her to him."

The judge chuckled. "I saw right off that those two were meant for each other. But I must say, my dear, you've given the town almost as much to talk about as the birth of the McCray triplets."

"Me? How?"

"Why, by selling the Potter Place to Megan's Uncle Dallas, of course. Nobody in town even knew you were interested in parting with any of your property."

"Neither did I. To tell you the truth, I didn't figure anybody would want it. Dallas sure took me by surprise, asking to buy the cottage."

"He's a good-looking fellow," the judge noted.

Beth Ann gave him a sharp tap him on the shoulder. "Don't you start playing matchmaker with me, Judge McCray. Just because you managed to get Megan and Daniel hooked up doesn't mean you're Barbourville's official cupid."

"Why, Miz Stanfield, you wound me, you really do." The judge clapped a hand to his heart and grinned impishly. Beth Ann sighed, then laughed out loud. Judge McCray was one of the most influential men in the county, and he was also one of the most meddling. Nothing gave him greater pleasure than interfering in the lives of his fellow citizens, but most of them had learned to be wary of his manipulations.

The judge turned and looked toward the back of Beth Ann's house. "Speaking of Dallas, where is the scoundrel? Megan sent me across the street to fetch him for lunch. You'd better come too. My dear wife and her Sunday school class brought enough food to Megan's this morning to feed half the town."

"And how is Miss Evelyn?"

"As feisty as always. You can see for yourself over lunch, just as soon as we find Dallas. Ah, here he comes around the corner of your house. I tell you, he sure doesn't look like a city boy these days."

Beth Ann looked Dallas' way and her eyes widened. He had donned a hard hat, which he quickly removed and dropped onto one of her lawn chairs. She moistened her lips. Funny how sexy Dallas had looked wearing that hard hat.

The judge waved an arm, motioning for Dallas to join them. "Come on, son. Chow's on across the street."

Dallas picked up his pace and was soon shaking the judge's hand. "Good to see you, sir. And that's welcome news about lunch. I'm starved." He quickly turned to Beth Ann. "You're joining us, aren't you?"

The judge spoke before Beth Ann could open her mouth. "Of course she is. Give her your arm and follow me." He stepped ahead of them across Redbud Road, and Beth Ann looked into Dallas' sparkling eyes, then joined him in a chuckle.

With a quick wink, Dallas extended his arm and Beth Ann allowed him to escort her across the street.

After lunch, which was a noisy affair that spilled out of Megan's kitchen and into the backyard, the crowd gradually drifted away. Beth Ann had purposely lingered because she'd seen so little of Megan lately, and when she finally started to say her good-byes, she quickly picked up signals that Megan wanted her to stay.

It was past time for her to get back to work,

but the shop could wait. Megan was her best friend, and if Megan wanted her to stay, then she would stay.

As soon as the last church lady waved goodbye and stepped out of the door, Megan grasped Beth Ann's arm and pulled her into the living room. Once there, she released Beth Ann and plopped down on the sofa. "Thank heavens for a moment when I can talk to you alone, Beth Ann. All this help I'm getting is about to drive me crazy but I can't say anything because I don't want to alienate Daniel's family and their friends." A tear slipped out of Megan's eye and slid down her cheek.

Beth Ann dropped onto the sofa and draped an arm around Megan's shoulder. "I'm so sorry, Meg. I guess we all just assumed you needed a lot of help with three little babies."

Megan wiped away the tear. "I suppose I did at first, and I still do somewhat, and I certainly wouldn't want everyone to stop coming around at all, so I can't say anything or . . . oh, I don't know, Beth Ann. Am I nuts or what?"

Beth Ann patted her shoulder. "You're a bit overwhelmed, my dear friend, and no wonder. Let me see if I can get the folks to cut back a bit. I suspect you could use less company and less food. Am I right?"

"Heavens, yes! But what can you do?"

"Don't you worry. I'll take care of everything."

"Oh thank you, Beth Ann. I'll be in your debt forever. I already owe you big."

"For what, may I ask?"

Megan grinned. "For selling your cottage to Uncle Dallas. I've never seen him this enthused about anything. You know how easily he gets bored."

"Good heavens, I don't deserve thanks for that. I haven't been this financially at ease in my life."

"Then you're glad that he decided to stay in Barbourville for a while?" Megan asked, a sly smile in her eyes.

Beth Ann cocked her head to one side and studied Megan's too-innocent expression. "Well, sure I'm glad he stayed. But why do you ask?"

Megan suddenly stilled and quickly held up a hand to silence Beth Ann.

Beth Ann sat quite still for a few seconds, then whispered, "What is it?"

"One of the girls is crying." Megan stood. "I'd invite you to visit the nursery but you probably need to get back to the shop."

"I'll take a rain check." She gave Megan a quick hug. "Call me if you need anything."

"Thanks. Whoops. Another girl just started yelling. I'll let you see yourself out." Megan waved as she dashed up the stairs.

* * *

The first thing Beth Ann did after leaving Megan's house was to visit the sheriff's office in hope of locating Daniel. Fortunately, he was in, but Dallas was with him, seated in a chair next to Daniel's desk. Both men looked up when Beth Ann walked in.

Daniel got to his feet. "Hello, Beth Ann. Is something wrong?"

"I just need to speak with you for a second."

Dallas stood. "I was headed to the cottage anyway. If you won't be too long, Beth Ann, I'll wait and walk you back that way."

Beth Ann fought to keep a pleased smile from slipping onto her face. "That would be fine. I'll just be a minute."

Dallas nodded. "I'll wait outside."

Daniel spoke as soon as the door closed behind Dallas. "What's up, Beth Ann?"

"Megan and I had a talk after lunch, and I told her I'd take care of a small problem she's experiencing. You need to call your family and their friends off, Daniel. Megan's had a little too much neighborliness lately."

Daniel's brows shot up. "But I thought Megan needed the help. And everyone else thinks the same."

"And she did need a lot of help at first. She doesn't need so much now. What she really needs is some time to herself. Having all those people around all the time is getting on her nerves. Tell them to back off. But they shouldn't drop her completely. Just no more food for a while, and no more than one person there in the mornings and one in the afternoon."

Daniel nodded. "I suspect you're right. Megan's been acting a little tense lately. But why didn't she say something to me?"

Beth Ann shook her head. "It's your family, Daniel, and your family's friends. Megan didn't want to alienate half the town. So you be careful what you say. I don't want anybody taking this out on Megan. Blame me if you need to, but not Megan."

Daniel smiled. "There's no need for blame. My folks will understand, I'll see to that. But thanks, Beth Ann. I appreciate it."

"Don't mention it. That's what friends are for." Beth Ann smiled, waved a quick good-bye, and hurried outside.

Dallas immediately stepped to her side. "Say, there's nothing wrong with Megan, is there? Or the girls?"

"Of course not. I would have told you immediately if anything was wrong with them. They're all fine. You're not having a problem at the cottage, are you?"

"You mean because I was visiting the sheriff's office? No. I just wanted to ask Daniel's advice about something. And you know what he told me?"

"What?"

"To ask your advice."

"My advice? About what?"

"Richard told me this morning that his partner, Eloise Smithfield, had stopped by the cottage to see how things are shaping up, and she said we ought to plan on getting some upscale work from local artisans for the finishing touches I'll need in order to make the cottage look authentic to this part of the country. But Richard didn't know who I should see, and he suggested I ask Daniel. And Daniel said you know practically everybody in the county and should be able to identify some good local artists."

Beth Ann cocked her head. "Mmmm. Well, come to think of it, I guess I do know a lot of people and some of them are fine artists. But it would help to know exactly what you need. You know, whether you want stained glass or pottery or watercolors, that sort of thing."

Dallas shrugged. "I don't know what I need. Would you take a look at the cottage with artwork in mind?"

"I'm no decorator, Dallas, but I'll be glad to tell you what I think."

"Great! Can you do it now?"

Beth Ann thought of her shop, then gave a mental shrug. She could afford to lose a little business, and she was eager to see what had been accomplished in the cottage. "Sure, I can go now."

Dallas smiled so broadly, Beth Ann felt her heart give a little leap. Darn but that man was good looking. She smiled back and fell into step beside him down Kessler Boulevard toward Redbud Road.

The cottage was not quite finished, but Dallas, Richard, and the workmen had made magnificent strides. They had built a new, wraparound porch, and the original porch had been enclosed to become an airy and bright foyer. The second Beth Ann stepped inside, she could visualize one of Hannah Phillips' stained glass pieces hanging in the west-facing window. On sunny days, rainbows of color would be cast on the white tile floor.

"What do you think?" Dallas watched her so closely, Beth Ann almost got the impression he was nervous about her reaction.

"It's a wonderful entranceway with tremendous possibilities. If you wanted to add some glass shelves to the east window there, I could line up some excellent hand-blown glass pieces you could display, along with a few green plants for contrast."

Dallas nodded. "I'll mention that to Richard. Now let me show you the rest of the house."

Cream-colored paint brightened the interior walls and contrasted nicely with the dark woodwork, which Dallas had cleaned, removing years of built-up smoke from the fireplace. The refinished hardwood floors shone golden throughout the house.

The heavy draperies were gone, and the sparkling clean windows sported white shutters that provided privacy but also allowed light to stream into the cottage.

The kitchen cabinets had been painted a soft yellow, and the sills of a bank of windows looking out into the side yard sported a fresh coat of white paint. A warm terra cotta tile floor spilled from the kitchen out onto an adjoining screened-in porch.

"Everything's wonderful, Dallas." Beth Ann couldn't believe he had transformed the old dark cottage into such a bright and appealing home. But she could see why Eloise Smithfield had suggested they add some art. The wall above the fireplace would be a perfect location for one of Mac Sharp's paintings of the nearby mountain peaks.

And interest could be added to the wall above the kitchen windows with a piece of Marsha Bennett's wire sculpture.

Beth Ann followed Dallas upstairs where she admired all of the changes he had initiated in the two bedrooms, the sewing room, and the relatively small bath. He allowed her to stand and simply stare around the rooms for as long as she needed in order to get a feel for the art that might work in each location.

Finally, when she decided she was through looking, she preceded him back down the stairs and paused in the kitchen. Dallas stepped in front of her and looked into her eyes.

"Okay, Beth Ann, I can almost see those wheels turning inside your head. Do you have any ideas about how I can use the work of local artists in order to put some finishing touches on the cottage?"

"Oh, I think so." Beth Ann smiled widely and tapped her toe. "I definitely think so. I'll start working on some of my ideas first thing in the morning."

Chapter Eight

Beth Ann spent the following morning on the phone with the artists she knew, asking what they had in stock and when she could come see it.

Most of the artists were people she had known since childhood, and she had kept up with them over the years. Beth Ann liked people, and she was liked in return. Everyone immediately invited her to stop by their houses or their workshops to inspect their stock.

She didn't invite Dallas to go along on her buying trip because she had a notion he would be confused by too many choices. Besides, he was still busy with last-minute work on the cottage.

She closed the shop on Thursday, borrowed a

pickup truck from Richard, and set off by herself to look over the stock of half a dozen artists. By 3:30 that afternoon, she was back with what she considered a treasure trove of art and fine crafts.

She pulled into the cottage's driveway around mid-afternoon and waved to Trevor, who obviously had come straight to the cottage after school. He hurried over to the driver's side of the pickup.

"Hey, Mom. Where did you get all this stuff?"

"I visited some friends and borrowed some of their artwork for Dallas to see so he can decide which pieces he wants to buy for the cottage. What are you doing here?"

"Mr. Vance said I could come over any time I wanted as long as there wasn't any dangerous work going on."

"That was nice of him. Where *is* Dallas?"

"I just got here so I don't know. Maybe he's inside. Yep, here he comes now."

Dallas stepped out of the front door and tossed his hand up. Trevor ran to meet him, and Beth Ann opened the truck door, then sat and watched as her son grabbed onto Dallas' hand and dragged him toward the pickup. A fond smile brightened Dallas' face, and Beth Ann's breath caught deep in her chest. It was hard to get her mind around the fact that a man like Dallas Vance existed. He was everything she could imagine wanting in a husband—kind, intelligent, sexy as all get-out, and good with her son. Too bad he was so far out of her league.

Dallas stepped to the side of the truck just as Beth Ann swung her legs around and started to slide off the high seat. He reached up to grasp her around the waist and then set her gently on the ground. He stood for a second, holding onto her waist and staring into her eyes, then leaned forward and planted a chaste kiss on her cheek before releasing her and turning to look into the bed of the truck.

"Good grief, woman! I've never seen such a load as you have here. You must have patronized every craftsman in this and all surrounding counties. Are those rocking chairs you have tied up back here?"

Beth Ann pulled a deep breath into her lungs and risked a quick glance at Trevor. She wondered what he thought about the kiss Dallas had given her, but he wasn't even looking her way. He was already trailing Dallas toward the back of the pickup. She gave a mental shrug and followed.

"I thought the rocking chairs would go nicely on your new screened-in porch. You don't already have furniture for it, do you?"

"No. I hadn't given it any thought yet, so thanks. What else do we have here?"

Beth Ann was amazed by the interest Dallas exhibited in every item she had packed into the back of the truck. He truly appreciated the workmanship that had gone into the pottery pieces she'd selected in anticipation of scattering them around the cottage. And he exclaimed over all four stained glass pieces she had brought for him to choose from. "You'll have to decide between them, I can't," he declared. "Any way we could keep them all?"

"I don't know," Beth Ann admitted. "I think only one of them would work in the entrance-way. Maybe I could identify another location or two if I walked through the cottage again."

"How about now? Do you have time?"

Beth Ann looked toward Trevor. "Are you hungry, sweetheart? I doubt you've had your after-school snack yet."

"You go ahead, Mom. I'll stop by the house and grab an apple."

"How about homework?"

"I got it all done at school. Jimmy Boland's dad put up a new basketball goal in their drive-way. Can I go shoot some hoops?"

"Fine, just be home in time for supper."

"Okay. Bye, Mr. Vance."

"Good-bye, Trev. Have fun."

"Sure thing." Trevor turned and hurried toward his own backyard.

Beth Ann waited until Trevor disappeared behind the lilac hedgerow, then turned to Dallas. "Have the workmen gone for the day? I don't want to get in anyone's way."

"Actually, what they were doing today was moving the furniture back, so everyone's gone now. Let's take the glass pieces inside with us. Having the furniture in place should help us decide where to hang them."

Thirty minutes later, Beth Ann and Dallas had decided on locations for three of the four pieces but there simply wasn't a window appropriate for the fourth one.

"Well, I can't let it go," Dallas declared. They had ended up in the kitchen, so he laid the final piece on the counter top and stood back to inspect it again. The colored glass depicted a cardinal perched in a dogwood tree with a spray of white blossoms in the background. "I know, I'll take it back to Chicago with me and hang it in one of the windows in my condo."

"That should be nice," Beth Ann said, wishing her stomach wasn't tying itself into knots at the thought of Dallas leaving. "Does your condo have windows that get plenty of sun?"

"On the west side, yes." He glanced up and frowned. "Say, you look tired. And no wonder.

You've probably been all over the county today on my behalf and as soon as you get back, I put you to work as my decorator."

He placed his hands on Beth Ann's shoulders. "You're something else, you know that?"

"What are you talking about?"

"Not only are you drop-dead gorgeous, but you're bright, well-spoken, and incredibly talented. I don't know anyone else who could have gone out and rounded up so many wonderful items that fit so perfectly in my cottage. Thank you a million times over, Beth Ann."

He leaned forward and his gaze dropped to her lips. Beth Ann felt her eyes widening. She could barely believe that Dallas was saying such wonderful things about her. She didn't think he was flattering her, so obviously he believed them. Which might explain why he was going to kiss her again and why she was going to let him.

She tilted her head back and waited with anticipation for his kiss. His lips were soft and warm and gentle, and Beth Ann felt the effects clear to the toes of her walking shoes. She wrapped her arms around him and reveled in the strength of his embrace. When he deepened the kiss, she reciprocated, pulling him close, wishing she could hold him forever and knowing she could not. But she would enjoy this moment, this kiss, this fantastic feeling of wholeness that she found only in his arms.

Dallas finally eased his lips away, but at the same time he pulled her closer in his embrace and murmured into her ear. "My beautiful Beth Ann, how on earth am I ever going to leave you? Being with you these last weeks has brought a meaning to my life that I've never experienced before. I've never felt this way with any other woman. It's as though you were created to fulfill all my—"

"Mom! Mom!"

Beth Ann leaped away from Dallas' embrace so quickly, both of them almost lost their balance. She turned to the front of the cottage, toward Trevor's voice, as fear gripped her, driving the breath from her lungs. She recognized that tone of voice. Something was wrong with her son.

Trevor appeared in the kitchen doorway before she had a chance to call out to him. He leaned against the door facing while tears ran in rivulets down his cheeks.

"Mom?" His voice trembled. "Mr. Vance? Something's going wrong with my leg, the one that was hurt in the accident."

Beth Ann reached him in two long strides. "What do you mean, baby?"

Dallas pulled a chair out from the kitchen

table. "Come here, buddy, and sit down. Then you can tell us what happened. Do you need any help?"

Trevor shook his head. "I can walk, but not without limping." As though to prove his words, he pushed off from the door facing and limped across the kitchen floor, then gingerly lowered himself into the chair Dallas had waiting. He held his left leg out stiffly in front of him.

Beth Ann hurried over and dropped to her knees beside him. "Trevor, baby, can you tell me what's going on?"

Trevor sniffed. "I'm sorry, Mom. I didn't want you to be out any more money on me."

"What are you talking about, sweetheart?"

"My leg's been bothering me for a while but I kept hoping it would get better. Then today, when we were shooting goals over at Jimmy's, I jumped for a rebound and when I came down, I could tell something was wrong."

Beth Ann reached with her bare hand to wipe the tears away from his cheeks. "Are you in a lot of pain, baby?"

He shook his head. "No, Mom, I'm only crying 'cause I feel so bad that I'm probably going to cost you a lot more money and time away from the shop, just like when I was hurt the last time."

Dallas pulled a handkerchief from his pocket and handed it to Trevor. "Then you can stop worrying, Trev. I've got this cottage finished and I'm at loose ends again. I'll help you and your Mom with whatever needs doing. Between the three of us, we can take care of everything."

Trevor nodded and swiped his face with Dallas' handkerchief. Then a tremulous smile touched his lips. "Thanks, Mr. Vance. That makes me feel a lot better."

It made Beth Ann feel a lot better too, although she knew it shouldn't. She knew perfectly well that to lean on Dallas now would only make her feel worse when he was no longer around to help her at times like this.

But for once, she was going to throw caution to the winds and lean on somebody else for a change.

Chapter Nine

Two hours later, Dallas and Beth Ann settled down at her kitchen table with cups of coffee. Dallas had purposely made it strong, and Beth Ann cradled hers in her hands as though she were chilled, despite the warm evening. Trevor sat between them, glancing first at his mom, then at Dallas. A frown pulled at his brows.

"You need to let me call Allen Marsh." Dallas stared hard at Beth Ann. He knew how independent she was, but he could also see from the stunned expression in her eyes that she was shaken to her very core.

She moistened her lips. "Megan's father, you mean?"

"Exactly. He'll know a specialist in Atlanta we can see, or he'll find one."

"Dr. Bentley didn't say we needed a specialist."

Dallas suppressed a sigh. He couldn't afford to let Beth Ann see how worried he was. She didn't need to be more frightened than she already was. But somehow he had to convince her to let him be of real assistance to her.

"Dr. Bentley is a good man," he said, careful to keep his tone even. "But he doesn't know why Trevor is limping. That means he doesn't know what to do. If Trevor's broken leg had healed properly, he shouldn't be limping now. Let me call Allen. He's lived in Atlanta since he was born, and he's led an active social life. He'll be able to get us in to see a specialist soon."

Beth Ann looked up from her coffee cup and into Dallas' eyes. The fear reflected in her gaze tugged at his heart. More than anything he wanted to assure her that he would take care of her, but he knew the quickest way to drive her away was to try to pull her too close. So he almost strangled on his coffee when she asked, "Will you go to Atlanta with me if we get an appointment?"

"Absolutely!" Dallas nodded slowly, as though his heart hadn't shifted into overdrive at the realization that Beth Ann trusted him enough to lean on him. "I'll call Allen on my cell phone right now."

Beth Ann nodded, then reached for Trevor's right hand. "Don't worry, baby. We'll find out what's going on."

Trevor placed his left hand on top of his mother's. "Don't *you* worry, Mom. Everything is going to be okay."

"I'll just step outside where the signal is stronger," Dallas said. He didn't want to intrude on this moment between Beth Ann and Trevor. Their mutual trust and love touched a place in him that he hadn't known existed, and he had made up his mind to help them if at all possible.

Fifteen minutes later when he stepped back inside the kitchen, Trevor was setting dishes out of the dishwasher onto the countertop and Beth Ann was putting them away. Both stopped what they were doing and stared at him.

"We're in luck," Dallas said. He looked first toward Trevor, then shifted his gaze to Beth Ann. "Allen is in the same club with one of the best orthopedists in Atlanta. He called the man at home and then called me back. He said Dr. Lowery told him that we can come to his office tomorrow afternoon. He'll work Trevor in."

Beth Ann pressed a hand to her stomach. "I can't believe everything's happening so fast. I don't even have gas in the car."

"You don't need gas. I'm driving and we're taking my car. I'm more familiar with it." Dallas was careful not to say that Beth Ann's car might not make it beyond the county line without breaking down, but she obviously recognized his motives. Her smile was wan, but it was a smile.

"Thanks, Dallas. I really do appreciate all this. What time do you think we should leave?"

"I'll pick you both up around ten in the morning. We should allow some extra time to find the office building. Can you be ready by ten?"

"We'll be ready," Beth Ann said, while Trevor nodded.

"Are you okay with all of this, Trev?" Dallas asked. He and Beth Ann were doing what needed to be done, but Trevor had said very little since they'd taken him to see the local doctor. Dallas worried that the boy might be feeling railroaded.

"I'm okay," Trevor said solemnly. "If something's wrong with my leg, I'd like to get it fixed as soon as we can."

"Okay, great." Dallas swallowed quickly. Darn if the boy wasn't mature for his age. "I'll see you in the morning then. Good night."

Dallas was aware that both Beth Ann and Trevor stepped to the door and watched him cross Redbud Road, so he paused on the sidewalk and turned to wave to them before he went inside to apprise Daniel and Megan of the latest plans.

By 5:00 the following afternoon, they were headed back up the interstate toward Tennessee. Beth Ann stared out of the passenger side window, watching bits and pieces of scenery flash by, barely aware that they had left the heavy traffic of Atlanta behind and were now traveling a rural stretch of I-75.

She was thankful that Trevor, who was worn out by the long wait to see the doctor, followed by numerous X-rays and other more sophisticated tests, had stretched out in the back seat and gone to sleep.

She was almost too exhausted herself to think clearly, but she knew she had to try. Surgery was called for, the doctor had said. The original break had not been set correctly, and unless they broke the leg again and reset it, Trevor was going to suffer intermittent pain. Worse, his left leg would be shorter than the other, causing increasing degrees of back pain in the future, along with other problems.

Poor Trevor. He had endured the afternoon and the ensuing news bravely, just as he had endured his original injuries bravely. He hadn't deserved any of this, and she couldn't help feeling guilty, even though she knew none of it was actually her fault.

But she was tired, tired of being afraid she would fail. She'd worked so hard ever since Trevor's daddy had died and left her alone. She liked to think she'd never let Trevor or anyone else see how terrified she was that she couldn't handle everything on her own.

She had tried to convince everyone that she was strong-willed and independent and fearless. Sometimes she had almost convinced herself.

And she wasn't sure that was a good thing.

She turned to look at Dallas and felt her heart give that familiar flip at the sight of his strong jaw line. He must have felt her gaze because he looked away from the road long enough to glance at her, then give her a quick smile.

"Penny for your thoughts," he said.

"I can't tell you how much your help means to me. I'm not sure I could have faced all of this alone."

Dallas took his right hand off the steering wheel and reached to grasp her left hand and give it a squeeze. "You won't ever have to face anything alone again, Beth Ann. I don't care where I am, you can always call on me."

"Thanks," Beth Ann murmured, then pulled her hand away and turned to look over her shoulder at Trevor's sleeping form. She and

Trevor's daddy had vowed to stand beside each other "for always" too, but she'd soon learned that "always" sometimes only lasted six months. She leaned her head back. "I think I'll try to sleep a while myself, if you don't mind. I didn't rest much last night."

"You go right ahead," Dallas said, just as she had known he would. "Why don't you recline the seat?"

Beth Ann followed his suggestion although she didn't really think she'd be able to go to sleep. She didn't wake up until he pulled in her driveway three hours later.

The doctor hadn't been able to schedule Trevor's surgery until Wednesday of the following week. Trevor would be in the hospital for five days, followed by three weeks of rehabilitation.

Beth Ann thanked her lucky stars that she hadn't given in to temptation and traded cars after she sold the cottage to Dallas. Now she had a decent amount of money in savings to help offset the costs of closing up the shop and staying in Atlanta for almost a month.

She got up earlier than usual the next morning and settled down with a cup of coffee to start making plans. She knew Daniel and Megan would look after the house while she was gone, and she could depend on Daniel and his deputy, Horace Barnhart, to keep an eye on the shop. Not that there was much crime in Barbourville, but it didn't hurt to take precautions. She'd have to remember to mention that to Daniel.

She figured she could stay in the hospital in Trevor's room for the first five days but she doubted they would allow her to hang around at night when they moved him to the rehab center. Maybe Megan's father could supply the name of a nearby hotel.

She reached for her bankbook and calculator. She could make an educated guess as to the daily cost of a hotel room. If she multiplied that by twenty-one days, then—

A soft knock on her kitchen door interrupted Beth Ann's thoughts. A smile tilted her lips. At this hour of the morning, it could be only Dallas. She stood and hurried to open the door.

Standing on her porch, a slight frown pulling at his distinguished forehead, was none other than Megan's father, Allen Marsh, who was one of the top attorneys in all of Atlanta.

"Mr. M-M-Marsh!"

"Good morning, Mrs. Stanfield. Dallas assured me you would be up when we saw your kitchen light on. I hope I'm not disturbing you."

"Not at all." Beth Ann stepped back and swung the door open. "Come in. Are Megan and the babies okay?"

A bright smile lit his face. "They're all wonderful. I still can't believe I have triplet granddaughters even though I should have realized it was a possibility. Megan's maternal grandmother had triplets. But you know that, being acquainted with Dallas and his brothers."

"Yes." Beth Ann bit her lip. If nothing was wrong at Megan's house, why had Mr. Marsh dropped by? She motioned toward the kitchen table. "Would you like a cup of coffee?"

"Thanks, but I'll take a rain check. I just wanted to give you this." He pulled a very small brown envelope from his pocket and laid it on the countertop.

"What is it?"

"Oh, I'm sorry. I thought Megan had already explained to you that I own a complex of condominiums near the rehab center. One of the units is vacant, and that's the key for it. The unit's yours for as long as you need it."

"Oh, well, ah, that's kind of you, sir, but I'm not sure I can afford a condo. I was thinking—"

"Please don't insult me by refusing my offer. I want you to use the place free of charge, Mrs. Stanfield." Allen Marsh set his jaw. "Megan has told me about how quickly you befriended her last summer when Judge McCray sentenced her to community service on those trumped-up charges. You also opened your home to her, and these kindnesses toward my only child comprise a debt I can never repay."

Beth Ann gulped, then nodded. "In that case, I'll accept the condo with heartfelt thanks."

"My card is in that envelope along with the key. My private number and my cell phone number are written on the back of the card. Call me anytime, night or day, if you should need me."

"Yes, sir."

"Call me Allen, please."

"All right, if you'll call me Beth Ann."

He stuck out his hand. "Deal. Now I've got to return to Atlanta for a meeting later today. I wish I could spend more time in Barbourville with my granddaughters, but I'll be back soon. Good day, Beth Ann."

Beth Ann shook his hand. "Good day, sir. I mean Allen."

He laughed before he turned and hurried down her porch steps and across the driveway to the black Mercedes waiting for him at the curb.

By the time Tuesday afternoon rolled around, Beth Ann was reeling from the support that had flowed in from the community. Hannah

Phillips, the stained glass artist, called to say that she and four other local artisans wanted to keep Beth Ann's shop open for her during the weeks she would be in Atlanta. When Beth Ann pointed out that they didn't have any experience with her bookkeeping methods or even with her cash register, Hannah said she wasn't to worry about that. They had already contacted Megan, who had helped Beth Ann in the shop last summer, and Megan had lined up babysitters so she could give the artists a crash course in running Beth Ann's shop.

Beth Ann finally agreed, but only on the condition that the artists bring some of their own wares to put up for sale in the shop so they wouldn't be neglecting their own livelihoods.

She was almost reduced to tears when Daniel informed her that he would be in Atlanta on Wednesday to sit with her and Dallas during the surgery. When she tried to object, he shushed her with a reminder that Megan would have his scalp if he wasn't there to support her best friend.

Since surgery was scheduled late on Wednesday morning, Dallas suggested they get up early and drive down that morning. Beth Ann agreed. She knew Trevor felt jittery about what he was facing, and she preferred keeping him in familiar surroundings for as long as possible.

Unfortunately, being in familiar surroundings wasn't helping her at all. Every time she thought about her son and surgery in the same breath, her heart fell to the pit of her stomach. Only when Dallas was with her did she feel any less frightened.

And the fact that he had insisted on driving them to Atlanta was the only thing that kept her sane that morning.

She had packed the evening before for herself and for Trevor, but she was up at 4:00 anyway, totally unable to sleep. She dressed, carried their suitcases to the kitchen, and put on a pot of coffee. She had drunk half a pot before it was time to get Trevor up, and by the time Dallas arrived an hour later, she was so wired she wouldn't have been surprised had she bounced to the door instead of walking.

Dallas reached for her hand. "Your hand is frigid. You need to try to relax a bit. Trevor has a wonderful and very experienced doctor. He couldn't be in better hands."

Beth Ann nodded. "I know. But he's just a little boy." Her voice broke. "He'll always be my little boy."

"Of course he will. And he wouldn't want it any other way, but he's also becoming a young man now. He worries about you, too, you know."

Beth Ann blinked rapidly. "I know, but I think

he worries a lot less since you're helping us with this trip and everything else. I can't tell you—"

Dallas held up a hand. "Then don't try. Besides, I think I hear Trev coming." He turned toward the sound of Trevor's footfalls. "Hey, young man. Are you ready? Great! Let's go then."

Chapter Ten

The following weeks would always remain a blur in Beth Ann's memory, although specific events forever burned crystal clear.

Such as the moment Allen Marsh and his two brothers stepped into the waiting room just before Trevor's surgery, having taken time out of their busy schedules to be there to provide moral support for Beth Ann.

Such as the moment when the doctor stepped into the waiting room to tell her that Trevor had come through the surgery just fine.

Such as the moment she watched Trevor take his first step on his repaired leg and declare there was no pain.

And always there was Dallas, often lurking in

the background as though trying to convince Beth Ann he wasn't hovering around her and Trevor, always on the lookout for some way he could be of benefit to either of them.

On several occasions, both at the hospital and later at the rehab center, Dallas had insisted she go back to the condo and rest while he stayed with Trevor.

And when Beth Ann wouldn't leave Trevor at mealtime, Dallas generally disappeared for a little while and then returned with a tray of food from the hospital cafeteria or a carry-out bag from a nearby fast food restaurant.

He was there, too, on the morning Trevor was released from the rehab center. He brought his car around to the admissions door, then jumped out and came around to help Trevor into the back seat. Dallas had provided a pillow and blanket in case Trevor needed to lie down. By the time they were half an hour up the road, Trevor was asleep.

Beth Ann leaned her head back against the headrest. "I can't believe it's finally over and we're going home. Everyone's been so nice, especially at the rehab center. I know Trevor was dreading that, but it worked out just fine for him."

"He's a brave young man." A fond smile lit Dallas' face. "Even the therapists seemed impressed with his willingness to push himself even when the exercises were painful."

"You were great with him too, Dallas. I think he may have pushed himself simply because you were there and he didn't want to disappoint you."

Dallas' eyebrows shot up. "Do you really think so?"

"I do. He's very fond of you, you know."

"Well, I'm very fond of him too."

Beth Ann grinned. "Yes, I could tell. And it's been good for Trevor to have a male role model taking such an interest in him."

"I think Trev and I have been good for each other." Dallas glanced at Beth Ann from the corner of his eye. "You look sleepy. Why don't you lay back in the seat until we get home?"

"I think I will rest for a few minutes. Not until we get home, I'm sure. But maybe for a little while."

Three hours later, when Dallas pulled into Beth Ann's driveway, she sat up and yawned. "Wow, I can't believe we're already here. Is Trevor still sleeping?"

Trevor spoke from the back seat. "Not any more. I just woke up. It sure is good to get home."

"I'll be around and help you out in a minute, buddy." Dallas cut the motor and opened his door. In less than fifteen minutes, he had Trevor comfortably situated in the parlor with the telephone nearby so he could start calling his friends to tell them he was home.

When Dallas returned to the kitchen, he found Beth Ann staring into the open refrigerator, a pleased smile brightening her face. "Bless Megan's heart! She's filled the fridge for me. There's potato salad and ham and fresh vegetables and tea. Are you hungry?"

"Just thirsty. I wouldn't turn down a glass of iced tea."

"Just a jiffy. Sit down at the table, unless you're tired of sitting. I'm sorry I conked out on you and didn't help with the driving."

"The driving was not a problem." Dallas walked over to the door. "I am a little tired of sitting, though. I'll carry in the luggage while you fix the tea. That will help me work some kinks out."

Ten minutes later he settled down at the kitchen table while Beth Ann placed a tall glass of iced tea in front of him, then sat down across from him. Dallas took a swallow of the sweet tea, then jiggled the ice cubes while a frown pulled at his brow. He opened and closed his mouth twice before he finally spoke. "Dayton called me last night."

Beth Ann sat up straighter. "Oh?"

"He needs me to come back to Chicago."

"When?"

"As soon as possible. I'll probably leave first thing in the morning."

Beth Ann swallowed. "I thought Dayton wanted you to stay in Barbourville for as long as possible. Is something wrong?"

"One of my clients needs some help, and he won't agree to letting either Dayton or Denver fill in for me. He's one of our biggest clients, and it could hurt the firm if he decided to go to someone else."

"I see." Beth Ann sighed, then forced a smile. "I'll miss you."

"You don't have to."

"What do you mean?"

Dallas reached across the table and grasped Beth Ann's hand. "Come with me, you and Trevor. You and I will get married and we'll make a life for the three of us in Chicago. We could start out living in my condo but if you would prefer, we'd look for a house in the suburbs. We could put Trevor in a private school if you think he'd like that. I'd see to it that he doesn't want for anything at all."

Beth Ann moistened her lips and slowly pulled a deep breath into her lungs. A proposal from Dallas was the last thing she had ever expected.

Of course she knew he was fond of her and Trevor. But she had never foreseen a proposal of marriage, perhaps because she knew marriage between them was simply not possible. She could never take Trevor away from Barbourville, away from his friends and the only home he had ever known.

Besides, Dallas was an urbane and highly educated attorney. While he might believe that he could be happy married to a woman with a high school education and a small-town level of sophistication, Beth Ann wasn't willing to take that chance. She had spent too much of her life fending for herself and her son to risk ending up as the dependent of a man who might someday be just a bit ashamed of her.

Dallas lifted his hand and pulled it back across the table. "You won't go with me," he said flatly.

Beth Ann bit her lip. "I can't, Dallas. It's not that I don't care for you, but—"

Dallas got to his feet. "It's all right, Beth Ann. I never really had much hope that you'd agree to my proposal. And I can't blame you. You and Trevor have roots here that go back a long way. As much as I'd love for us to form a family, I can't blame you for not taking Trevor away from all he's known."

Beth Ann also stood, then walked around the table and wrapped her arms around Dallas. "You know I care for you," she said, surprised to realize just how deep her feelings ran.

He pulled her closer. "Hey, it's not like I'm leaving for good. I still own that cottage in your backyard. Which reminds me."

Beth Ann pulled back and looked up into his face. "Reminds you of what?"

"I've been running an ad in the Atlanta paper for the past few days, and I've already got a renter lined up for next week. I thought I'd be around to handle the details, but since I won't, could I give you a percentage of the rental in return for you meeting the folks, passing along the keys, and showing them where everything is located? I'd consider it a personal favor."

"I'd be happy to take care of it for you, but you don't have to pay me."

"I insist. I'd have to pay a rental agent, assuming I could find one, and you're much more knowledgeable about the cottage than anyone else I could find. I'll just leave you the people's names, and you can take your twenty percent when they pay on arrival."

"All right. What's the weekly rental?"

"Twelve hundred."

"As in dollars?"

"Is that a little low, do you think?"

Beth Ann gulped. "No, I guess not. Probably it's just about right."

"Good. Then I'll jot down all the details tonight and leave my notes and the keys with

Megan to give to you tomorrow. I have to leave very early in the morning, so I probably won't see you then. Do you mind if I say good-bye to Trev on my way out?"

"Of course not. He'll hate to see you go, so be sure and remind him that you'll be back."

Dallas nodded. "I'll most definitely be back. In the meantime, if you have any problems with the cottage, give me a call. Good-bye, Beth Ann."

"Good-bye." She picked up their tea glasses and carried them to the sink. It was very important, she had decided, to keep Dallas from seeing the tears that were building in her eyes. She didn't want him comforting her. She was too afraid that if he ever put his arms around her again, she wouldn't let him leave without her.

Chapter Eleven

Beth Ann woke up early the next morning, grabbed her robe, and hurried downstairs to the kitchen. She pulled back the curtain and looked across the street. Dallas' car no longer sat at the curb, but she had known before she looked out that he was gone.

Town felt empty. She felt empty.

She also felt a bit angry with herself. She couldn't believe she'd grown so accustomed to having Dallas around. Ever since the day she'd lost Trevor's daddy, she'd been careful not to need anyone too much.

She shrugged and turned away from the window. Dallas was gone and it was time to get on with her life. She needed to check her bank accounts. Her savings had been depleted by Trevor's most recent medical bills and she knew she would be in debt again. She now needed to figure out just how bad it was going to be.

She had barely finished pouring water into the drip coffeemaker when the telephone rang. Who could be calling this early? She hurried across the room to the wall phone and grabbed the receiver. "Hello?"

"Good morning."

"Dallas?"

"Yes. Did I wake you?"

"No, I was making coffee. Where are you?"

"About a hundred miles up the road. I waited to call until I got out of the mountains and could get a strong enough signal for my cell phone. I wanted to say that I already miss you."

Beth Ann gulped. "Is something wrong?"

"As a matter of fact, there is. It suddenly dawned on me that I had forgotten something extremely important."

"Oh, I'm sorry. What did you forget?"

"I forgot to tell you I love you, and I apologize for that. I asked you to marry me without telling you how much I love you. Not that I expect you to change your mind about coming with me. But I just wanted you to know."

Beth Ann sat down hard in the straight chair next to the telephone.

"Beth Ann? Are you still there?"

"I'm here."

"Good. I thought I'd lost the signal. Or are you just speechless?"

Beth Ann laughed. "You sure know how to wake a gal up, Dallas Vance."

"It's good to hear your voice. Say, I left all my phone numbers with Megan to give to you. Cell phone, business phone, home phone, et cetera. Any time you need me or have a question about the cottage or just want to talk, call me."

"I will."

"Did Trev have a good night?"

"He slept straight through, and he's still asleep."

"That sounds good. Tell him I said hi."

"Yes, I'll do that."

"Good-bye, Beth Ann."

" 'Bye, Dallas."

He cut the connection and Beth Ann slowly placed the receiver back on the hook and sat for several seconds just staring at the far kitchen wall.

So Dallas loved her.

She hadn't thought about love in years, not in the way Dallas meant. She had assumed she would never know that kind of love again and it felt strange, knowing a man loved her.

But did she love him? Obviously she was attracted to him and had been from the first time she'd laid eyes on him. But love?

Love was a whole different ballgame from attraction. Attraction was fun, dazzling, mystifying—a wild carnival ride at midnight when the stars were out and the sky was black and you were dizzy from spinning around in circles.

But love! Ah, love was so much more. It was a warm feeling in the pit of your stomach when you heard his voice on the other end of the phone line. It was a jarring leap of your heart when he walked into a room. It was a deep, quiet, slow journey down paths that led from giddiness to profound trust.

Did she love Dallas? And if she did, would she have the courage to admit it to herself, let alone to him?

Beth Ann pushed herself to her feet and crossed the kitchen to pour herself a cup of coffee. She wasn't going to think about love anymore this morning. She had some time before she needed to head to the shop so she would check on the cottage and make sure everything was ready for Dallas' renters when the first of the week rolled around. She would keep busy, and she would think about love some other day when she was stronger and less shaken by Dallas' absence.

*   *   *

She checked on Trevor, saw that he was still sleeping, and left a brief note stuck to his bedroom door telling him that she was going to check on the cottage. When she stepped outside, she realized how much the weather had changed in the weeks she had been away.

She was greeted by a sharp chill in the air and a light breeze that rattled the yellowing maple leaves and sent dozens of them floating through the air. A layer of brown leaves covered the ground and hid the path leading to the cottage. Beth Ann made a mental note to call Mikie Smith and see if he would have time to work in her yard after he finished with Daniel's. Since she was getting the commission on the cottage, she would use the money to get both yards raked.

The musty smell of fall wafted up from the crunching leaves beneath her feet, taking her back in time to the days when Trevor had been a little boy and she had raked up piles of leaves just so he could jump in them and scatter them to the winds again. He wouldn't quit until he was so tired she had to pick him up and carry him into the house.

How wonderful it would be to have another child playing in the falling leaves someday.

Beth Ann stopped in her tracks. Where had that thought come from? Sure, she was young enough to have another child. She'd only been nineteen when Trevor was born after all. But she had long ago given up on thoughts of having a family beyond her and Trevor.

She shrugged, then sighed. She refused to allow her thoughts to wander down that path. Instead, she stepped off again, heading around the corner of the cottage and stopping to admire the deep wraparound porch Dallas had added after enclosing the old one for a brighter entry hall.

The porch sported a wooden swing on one end and a park bench on the other. It was attractive but not welcoming in Beth Ann's opinion. She cocked her head to one side and studied the area for a few seconds. Something seasonal was needed, she decided. Something like a few gourds and pumpkins to decorate the concrete porch steps and the porch posts. She would look into purchasing some fall produce when she went into town to open the shop later in the morning.

She wasn't sure what had gone on in the store while she was away. She had called two or three times from Atlanta, and always one of her friends had answered and assured her that everything was under control.

Suddenly eager to check on her shop, she turned and hurried through the rustling leaves, back to her house. She couldn't leave until she was sure Trevor was up and about. Thanks to the therapy he had undergone, he moved about easily on his crutches but she didn't want to trust him in the kitchen yet. She'd just see to it that he had a healthy breakfast before she ran into town. Trevor would be fine by himself for a couple of hours.

An hour and a half later, Beth Ann hurried down the sidewalk on Kessler Boulevard headed toward her shop. Her progress was slow because everyone she met stopped her to inquire about Trevor's health and to ask if she needed anything. She was touched by the honest concern of her neighbors and was reminded again of why she preferred small-town life.

When she neared the shop, she couldn't help but notice a small group of strangers—obviously tourists—gathered outside her display window, which was rare. Most tourists had little interest in the mid-line clothes Beth Ann carried in her shop.

One woman in the group pointed toward something in the window, another woman nodded, and one of the men opened the door to Beth Ann's Place and stepped back. Everyone trooped in.

Beth Ann purposely slowed down so the strangers could enter her shop while she lagged behind to try to figure out what had attracted their attention. When she arrived in front of the window, she stood staring inside, trying to figure out what they'd been pointing at.

Her mannequins, as usual, sported outfits that were for sale inside. Someone had dressed them in her new winter merchandise, which she appreciated, but there was nothing out of the ordinary in their corduroy slacks and coordinated pullover sweaters.

Then she realized that one of the mannequins was seated in a rocker just like the ones she had found for Dallas to use on the cottage's screened-in porch. And back in the corner of the display window, almost hidden from view, sat a small table covered by a hand-woven shawl. In the center of the table stood a pottery vase boasting a delicate green glaze, and sitting on the floor around the table were a large wooden bowl and some smaller pottery pieces.

While Beth Ann watched, Hannah Phillips stepped into view, picked up the wooden bowl, and turned back toward the inside of the store. Beth Ann had insisted that Hannah and the other artists place some of their pieces in the shop while they were sitting in for Beth Ann. Wouldn't it be wonderful if their good deed in helping her out was also helping them increase their sales?

Not wanting to intrude on Hannah and the

tourists, Beth Ann tarried outside until the group of strangers exited ten minutes later carrying two large shopping bags. They chattered in excited tones about the pieces they had bought, discussing where in their homes they would place their new purchases or which family member would be the recipient of a particular item when Christmas rolled around.

Beth Ann watched them stroll down the street. Then she turned and hurried into her shop. She was looking forward to thanking Hannah for her help, but Hannah rushed forward to envelop Beth Ann in a hug.

"It's good to see you back," Hannah said. "Sheriff McCray stopped by this morning and told me you and little Trevor were back and that your boy is doing just fine. I'm so thankful."

"Thanks, Hannah." Beth Ann returned the hug, then stepped back. "I hope my shop hasn't been too much of a burden for you and the others while I was gone."

"Heaven help us, child. It's been a true blessing for every one of us. We didn't ever think about selling our art and crafts in town. We always just depended on craft shows, but they're few and far between. Why, I've sold more of my stained glass pieces these past four weeks than in the rest of the year put together."

"You have no idea how happy I am to hear

that, Hannah." Beth Ann glanced around at her shop. Obviously the artists had not wanted to upstage her merchandise and so had kept their wares in the background, sitting on small tables tucked into the corners or hanging high on the walls. She couldn't help but wonder how much more they might have sold if they'd displayed their art more prominently.

Suddenly, a thought occurred to Beth Ann. Perhaps there was a way she could help the artists and herself at the same time. After all, selling clothes was never going to provide her with a decent living.

She'd have to think about it, of course. It wouldn't do to jump into something without knowing what she was doing.

She looked back at Hannah, who was observing her with a slight frown. "Your shop does look a mite different than it did when you left," Hannah said, her frown deepening. "I surely hope you don't think we've taken too many liberties with everything."

Beth Ann reached to grasp her hand. "Heavens no, Hannah. I love the way you've integrated your art with my merchandise. In fact, I'd like to talk to you someday soon about an idea that's occurred to me. But right now, I'm hoping you'll stay in the shop for the rest of the morning so I can buy some pumpkins and gourds to decorate the cottage porch. Dallas' renters are due soon and I want to have the place looking nice for them."

Hannah grinned. "Sounds to me like you need to run by the farmer's market and then get on back home so you can take care of that boy of yours and the cottage too. I'll stay in the shop the rest of the day."

"You're sure you don't mind?"

"Mind? Child, I haven't enjoyed myself this much in years. Why, the tourists are just the most entertaining folks you've ever seen. Besides, Jeffrey Martin is supposed to come by right after lunch to bring more spoons, and he'll be expecting me to be here."

"You mean the Jeffrey Martin who carves those fantastic spoons and forks?"

Hannah nodded. "None other. I know his work is in short supply because it's so popular, but he liked the idea of us artists selling our wares in one place and he wanted to be a part of it. I've got orders for ten of his wooden spoons if he has that many today. Jeffrey's one of those folks who won't be rushed, but his work is all the better for that."

"Okay." Beth Ann was finding her idea more appealing by the minute, but she still needed time to think before she voiced it aloud. "I sure appreciate you keeping the shop open for the rest of the day."

"Now, child, don't give it another thought. Your boy needs you. You run along and take care of him."

Beth Ann smiled. "Will you be here tomorrow?"

"Sure will. Come in as late as you like."

"Okay, see you then. In the meantime, call if you need me." Beth Ann let herself out the shop door and paused to stare into the show window, trying to visualize how it might look if she proceeded with her idea. She had turned to walk away when four ladies she recognized as tourists hurried up the sidewalk.

"Here it is," one said, grasping another's arm and pulling her to a stop in front of the store. "Beth Ann's Place. You'll love the pottery. Come on, let's go in."

Beth Ann stepped back and let the four women pass her on their way into the shop. Then she smiled to herself and headed toward the small farmer's market to get what she needed for the cottage porch.

She and Trevor had finished dinner and were clearing the table that night when Dallas called. Trevor had been closer to the phone and had grabbed the receiver. Beth Ann could judge from his tone that he was thrilled to be hearing from Dallas.

"Yes, Mr. Vance, I'm doing real good." Trevor smiled and nodded. "Yes, I'm doing my exercises just like they told me. I'm feeling fine. Okay, I sure will. Thanks! Here's Mom."

Beth Ann took the receiver and lowered herself into the chair by the phone. It felt good, knowing Dallas thought enough of them to call so soon. "Hey, there," she said. "How was your trip?"

"Uneventful, thank goodness. It's great to hear your voice. Is Trev doing as well as he sounds?"

"I think so, yes."

"And how are you?"

"Good," Beth Ann said. "I had a nice time getting the cottage ready for your renters. I'm just adding a few seasonal decorations to the outside. I hope you don't mind."

"Of course not. Buy anything you want and take it out of the rent."

Forty-five minutes passed by the time Beth Ann and Dallas said their good-byes. He promised to call again soon to see if the renters had arrived and gotten settled in. Beth Ann promised she'd let him know if any problems arose before he called.

When she finally placed the receiver back on its hook, she paused to analyze the way she felt:

Giddy, ecstatic, elated, delighted. None of the adjectives were adequate to describe how she felt. Which could mean only one thing.

She was in love.

She was in love with a man who was in love with her, and they were miles apart, in much more than distance.

She stared across the room, thinking. There were a thousand reasons why she and Dallas could never be together, not the least of which was her unwillingness to marry a man who was so much better educated than she.

And of course she would never force Trevor to move away from his home and his friends.

But love, she knew, didn't come calling too many times in one lifetime, and so surely it must be worth fighting for.

On the other hand, some battles simply couldn't be won. However much she and Dallas might be right for each other, the circumstances were wrong in so many other ways. No doubt it would be best all around if she simply decided to let him go and get on with her life.

She stood and stepped out into the hallway. The lights were on in the parlor, and she could hear the television playing.

She squared her shoulders. It was time to have a talk with her son.

Chapter Twelve

Dallas' tone at the other end of the phone line was clearly exasperated. "I understand what you're saying, Beth Ann. You know I don't agree with you, but I'm not going to fight you on this any longer. If you want us to remain friends, so be it. I hope you'll continue to manage the cottage for me though. The last three renters had nothing but praise for all of your arrangements, especially the homey way you decorated everything."

"The decorating is a pure pleasure for me." Beth Ann had answered the phone in the parlor where she'd been deeply engrossed in her reading. She laid her book on the floor beside her chair and slung her leg across the overstuffed chair arm, prepared to settle back for a long chat with Dallas. "I haven't had the time or money to spend on decorating my own house in years, but since I can take the cost of decorations for the cottage out of the rent, I'm both enjoying myself and halfway supporting some of the artists and small farmers around here."

"You know that's fine with me. Did I tell you the cottage has been rented for the two weeks prior to Thanksgiving by a family from Ohio?"

"Ohio? Are you advertising nationwide now?"

"I'm not advertising at all. This appears to be a word-of-mouth situation. The Ohio family is related to the renters from Atlanta who were there two weeks ago."

"I guess you were right when you said people love cottages these days. Why don't you e-mail me the details?"

"I will. Say, you wouldn't be able to come to Chicago and go to a charity ball with me, would you? I'd really love to show you my city."

Beth Ann straightened in the chair. "When is it?"

"A week from Friday. I'll send you the plane fare if you'll come."

"Frankly, I could swing the fare myself considering how much commission I'm earning from your rentals. But I'm really sorry, Dallas. I, ah, I just can't make it a week from Friday."

"No problem. I understand. I'd better go. Denver's expecting me to meet him for a movie. Tell Trev hello for me."

"Sure. 'Bye." Beth Ann hung up the phone and fought back tears. Would she have gone to Chicago if she didn't have class a week from Friday? She liked to think she would have. She needed to broaden her horizons. Besides, she could close her eyes and picture herself twirling across the dance floor in Dallas' arms while wearing one of Megan's designer gowns and those beautiful strappy evening shoes that Megan had shown her one time.

Megan would be delighted to loan her everything she could possibly need for the trip. After all, now that Megan was a wife and mother instead of an Atlanta socialite, she had little use for the magnificent designer clothes, shoes, handbags, and luggage she had owned before she married Daniel.

Yes, Beth Ann could envision it all. She'd borrow Megan's blue evening gown, the one with the swirls of sequins around the hem, and when Dallas twirled her . . .

Her eyes popped open and she gasped in horror. Her imagination had suddenly shifted gears so that she had been picturing a different woman in Dallas' arms. A woman who was slinky and alluring. A woman who was beautiful and sophisticated.

The truly terrible thing was that this other woman might become a reality if Beth Ann didn't go to Chicago.

She reached for the phone. Somehow or another she would find a way to make up that class she had scheduled for a week from Friday. She quickly dialed Dallas' number.

Beth Ann couldn't believe the size of O'Hare Airport. To say she was terrified was putting it mildly. Her mouth was so dry she couldn't even moisten her lips, which felt as though they were cracking after being exposed to the arid cabin air in the long flight from Atlanta.

And how would she ever find her way out of the airport and to her hotel if Dallas wasn't there to meet her?

She blew out her breath in a deep sigh of relief. She could see him now, waiting for her, his eyes scanning the crowd. She knew the second he saw her because a wide smile brightened his face and he threw up a hand in greeting. She barely refrained from running and flinging herself into his arms.

He, fortunately, was less inhibited. He hurried up to her, placed his hands on her shoulders, and bent to kiss her quickly on the lips. "Hi, gorgeous," he murmured. "Welcome to Chicago." Then he pulled her into a warm hug.

Beth Ann hugged him back. It felt so wonderful, so right to be back in his arms again. She felt truly safe for the first time since she'd left home early that morning.

Dallas ended the hug but reached for her hand. "How was your flight?"

"Okay. I'm glad to be on the ground though."

"And I can't tell you how happy I am to have you here. Denver and Dayton both want to see you, so I've let Denver make reservations for all of us at a restaurant tonight. And, as I told you on the phone, you'll be staying in a hotel not too far from my condo. Denver wanted to make you a reservation at a B&B, but I told him you might prefer something a bit different while you're here. After all, you're quite accustomed to living in an older house. So is a hotel okay with you?"

Beth Ann managed to nod even though her head was spinning. "Sounds great. What else is on our schedule, besides the dance on Saturday evening?"

"I thought I'd let you decide. Since you came a little early, we can sightsee all day tomorrow and part of the day on Saturday if you'd like.

There are the museums and the planetarium and the aquarium and the zoo and—"

"Whoa!" Beth Ann laughed. "That all sounds wonderful but it's probably too much for a couple of days, and I really would like to get a feel for the city. Could we just drive around a little bit? I think I'd enjoy seeing some of the different neighborhoods."

"Absolutely. Why don't we swing by your hotel first and let you freshen up if you'd like."

"Sounds wonderful to me."

"Great. Then let's go get my car and we'll get out of here. On the way to the hotel, you can tell me how Trevor's getting along and how you ever managed to get out of Barbourville without him."

Twenty-five minutes later, Dallas escorted Beth Ann into a hotel that was much more luxurious than any she had ever patronized before. But that was fine with her. When she had called Dallas to accept his invitation to come to Chicago, he had insisted on paying all of her expenses since he would be the host. For once, Beth Ann had swallowed her pride and given in gracefully. After all, she suspected this would be the only time she would be able to visit Dallas in Chicago and she wanted it to be special.

Because however impossible their future together might be, they wouldn't be losing touch with each other. Dallas would be coming back to Barbourville to visit Megan and her girls and to check on the cottage. If there could be nothing else between them, Beth Ann hoped she and Dallas would remain friends, and she wanted to know more about how he lived, to become a bit familiar with his world at least this one time.

So she hadn't complained when he'd reserved her tickets in first class, and she didn't object at all when she discovered that he'd paid a shuttle service to pick her up at home and drive her to the Atlanta airport.

Now, as she registered at the bustling reservations desk, she couldn't help but enjoy the understated respect she was shown by the staff. And when the bellhop glanced at the luggage she'd borrowed from Megan and quickly tipped his hat, she couldn't suppress a slight smile. The young man had no way of knowing that if Beth Ann had entered the hotel toting her own ratty suitcase, she would likely have been tossed out on her ear.

Dallas accompanied her to the suite he'd reserved for her, inspected the rooms to make sure all was in order, and tipped the bellhop before offering to wait downstairs while she freshened up.

"Don't be silly," Beth Ann told him. "You can wait out here on the sofa while I brush my teeth and run a comb through my hair. Can I come back later and change clothes before we meet your brothers for dinner?"

"Sure. In the meantime, I'll show you around the Windy City."

Five hours later, Beth Ann had fallen in love with Chicago. The city was a study in contrasts, although she suspected Dallas had refrained from showing her the seamiest side of the city.

Still, they had covered a tremendous amount of ground, driving through neighborhoods that boasted some of the city's most impressive historic homes and mansions. They had visited The Field Museum, which was absolutely the most amazing place Beth Ann had ever seen. From there they went to the Adler Planetarium, which she also enjoyed, but by that time her long day was catching up with her.

"I'm more than ready to go back to the hotel and put my feet up for a while," Beth Ann declared when they got back into Dallas' car. "How about you?"

"That's fine with me. I'll drop you off and go on home to clean up, then come back and pick you up for dinner."

"Could I see your condo sometime while I'm here?"

"We should be able to work that in tomorrow."

Beth Ann nodded. "Good. Trevor wants me

to describe everything for him when I get back, and he especially mentioned your condo."

"That's interesting. I wonder why?"

Beth Ann shrugged. "I think he's just interested in how you live. You've become a role model for him, you know."

"That's quite a responsibility. I hope I never let him down."

"I don't think you need to worry about that. You're good with him."

"Thanks! Maybe he can come visit me here next summer when he's not in school."

"I think he'd like that. By the way, how should I dress for dinner tonight?" She was a bit worried that they'd be going to some fancy French place where she couldn't even read the menu.

"Dress casual. Denver made our reservations at a small Italian place in his neighborhood. They make the best lasagna you've ever sunk a tooth into."

Beth Ann grinned. "You've been hanging around Barbourville too long."

"What do you mean?"

"Picking up expressions like *sunk a tooth into*."

Dallas grinned too. "I like the language I hear in Barbourville, thank you very much. In fact, I've found a lot of things in Barbourville that I like."

He had pulled the car to a stop in front of the

hotel and turned to Beth Ann as though he planned to say more, but the doorman had already hurried over and opened her door.

"You don't need to come up with me, Dallas," she said. "Just give me a call when you head back this way."

He nodded. "Okay, I'll talk to you later."

Beth Ann was a little leery about having dinner with Dallas' brothers. She'd never spent much time with either of them, but she knew that Dayton tended to be quite formal while Denver was private to the point of almost appearing withdrawn.

Fortunately for Beth Ann's peace of mind, both men seemed to go out of their way to charm her that evening. The restaurant Denver had chosen was noisy and crowded and totally enjoyable. The food was just as good as Dallas had promised, and Beth Ann found herself laughing so hard she had to dab tears away from her eyes.

Finally, when they had finished their tiramisu but still lingered over their decaf coffee, Dayton asked, "What do you young people plan to do tomorrow?"

Denver grimaced. "You mean while the elders of the tribe, like you, rest from your labors?"

Dayton lifted one brow. "There's no need for

sarcasm, my dear brother. I was merely making conversation."

Dallas heaved a sigh. "I should have known all this brotherly harmony was too good to last. Shut up, both of you. To answer your question, Dayton, Beth Ann and I are going to continue our sightseeing in the morning by going to the aquarium. Then we'll probably pick up lunch somewhere and take it back to my condo. Beth Ann has to take a report back to Trevor about where I live."

Beth Ann chimed in. "And then I'll need to go back to my hotel to allow time to get ready for the dance. To tell you the truth, guys, I'm more than a little nervous about going to something that's called a charity ball. Will there be a lot of dignitaries there?"

The three men glanced at each other. Their gazes held just long enough for Beth Ann to suspect that they'd managed to communicate something between the three of them. Then Dayton quickly turned to her with a too-bright smile.

"Oh, probably just the mayor and a few others, but there's absolutely nothing for you to worry about. The Vance triplets will be there to make sure you have a good time."

"You mean you and Denver are going too? I didn't know that."

"What? You mean Dallas didn't tell you?

Denver and I are on the board of directors just the same as Dallas. We wouldn't miss this for the world."

"Great," Beth Ann said, smiling at each brother in turn. She would have bet half of what little she owned that neither Dayton nor Denver had entertained the least notion of going to the ball until she'd mentioned her fears.

Beth Ann was convinced that Cinderella could not have felt any more special than she did by the time she was ready for the dance that evening.

First of all, even before she left Barbourville, Megan had talked her out of wearing the dress with the sequins around the hem. Instead, Megan had gone to her closet and pulled out what she said was the perfect dress for Beth Ann—a midnight blue floor-length chiffon with a nipped-in waist and low-cut bodice. Megan also passed along the matching shoes and a gorgeous beaded evening bag.

The dress' dark color, Megan claimed, emphasized the porcelain-like beauty of Beth Ann's skin and highlighted the auburn strands intermingled with her red hair. A diamond brooch pinned high on the bodice added a touch of sparkle to the ensemble.

Megan's final gift to Beth Ann had been a

hair appointment in the hotel's salon, which she had scheduled for late that afternoon. Although Beth Ann was half intimidated by the thought of putting herself in the hands of a city hair stylist, she forced herself to go, knowing Megan would be disappointed in her if she didn't.

Still, when she discovered that the Lynn who was to do her hair was a man, she almost turned and fled. After all, she'd mostly trimmed her own hair for years, and the few times she'd been to the beauty parlor, only her high school pal Sarah had ever touched her hair.

Fortunately, the minute Lynn laid eyes on her, he started raving about the beauty of her hair—its rare color, its texture, even its unruly tendency to curl in all sorts of different directions.

By the time she left the salon and returned to her room, Beth Ann had promised to come back in an hour and allow Lynn to apply her makeup for her. She hurried to the bedroom in her suite and stared at herself in the mirror. Lynn had trimmed her hair a bit, then piled it on top of her head while leaving several strands hanging around her face.

She sighed, but it was a happy sigh. She had a feeling that by the time Dallas came to pick her up tonight, she was going to feel even more special than Cinderella.

The expression of admiration on Dallas' face

when she opened the door to him that evening brought a smile of relief to her face. And later, at the ball, Dayton's and Denver's fulsome compliments convinced her that without a doubt, she looked as nice in her borrowed finery as any woman there.

In fact, she noticed several women staring at her as though they were trying to figure out who she was.

And no wonder. She was the center of attention from the three handsome Vance brothers. She had entered the ballroom on Dallas' arm, but Dayton was waiting for them and hurried to her side, claiming the first dance as soon as the orchestra warmed up.

Dallas had pretended to be furious that his brother had beat him to the punch, but his eyes had twinkled when he declared he would give in gracefully only if Beth Ann swore to save the second dance for him.

Then Denver strolled in. He nodded absently to several people who appeared to be seeking his attention. He then proceeded straight to Beth Ann's side and grasped her hand.

"Hello, lovely lady. Am I too late for the first dance?"

Dallas spoke up quickly. "Yes. And for the second one also. Do you want to claim the third?"

"I do." He lifted Beth Ann's hand to his lips. "Will you honor me with the third dance, my lady?"

Beth Ann giggled. "My three Prince Charmings," she said with a wide smile. "I adore each and every one of you."

"Then my love is not unrequited after all," Dayton declared, stepping to her side. With a phony frown, he reached to disengage Denver's hand from Beth Ann's. "Go away, little brother. My dance is about to begin."

Beth Ann's cheer subsided when Dayton led her out onto the dance floor. She'd been dreading this moment since she'd agreed to visit Dallas. Of course she and Jim had danced together at their high school proms, but neither of them had been especially adept. Thank goodness Megan had anticipated Beth Ann's fears and had tutored her a bit. Beth Ann only hoped she didn't embarrass herself.

Fortunately, all three of the Vance brothers were such good dancers, they easily swept Beth Ann around the floor and somehow kept her from stepping on their feet. She found it easy to adjust to each man's stride, and by the time Denver was leading her back to Dallas' side, she was relaxed enough to admit that she was actually enjoying herself.

That was true up until a break in the dancing

when a large and distinguished gentleman approached them and Dallas introduced her to the president of one of the largest companies in Chicago. On his heels were a trio of attorneys and two medical doctors, all of whom seemed intent on being introduced to Beth Ann.

Strangely, instead of feeling tongue-tied, as she had feared, Beth Ann found herself talking with each man as though she had just settled down to visit with a neighbor back in Barbourville.

By the time the evening was over, she was sorry to see it end. Never, in all her wildest dreams, had she ever imagined herself mingling with high society in Chicago and feeling so at ease. Not once during the evening had her lack of formal education presented an impenetrable barrier for her.

It was good to know that she could fit into Dallas' world in some respects. In others, of course, she couldn't. However much she might love him, however much she might love his city, her first obligation was to her son, and she simply could not take Trevor away from the only home he had ever known.

Nor, truth be told, did she think she could be happy living in a city, no matter how wonderful it might be. When she had visited Dallas' condo that morning, the view from his tenth-floor balcony had taken her breath away, but she knew she would miss walking down the five steps from her porch and being among trees and flowers and grass, even when the grass was too tall and the trees were shedding leaves she would have to rake up and cart off.

So she should have been relieved, she supposed, that Dallas barely touched her that evening when he took her back to the hotel. He had escorted her up to her suite, waited while she unlocked the door, and then planted the very briefest of kisses on her lips.

"Thank you for the evening," he said. He smiled but his eyes looked a bit sad. "I had a wonderful time. I'll call tomorrow before I come by to take you to the airport."

"Don't you want to come in for a while?" Beth Ann had asked. "I promised Trevor I'd call him and tell him all about the evening. He would love to talk to you too."

"Thanks, but I've got some work I need to take care of. I'll see you tomorrow."

Beth Ann watched him walk down the hall, then turn to wave at her. She waved back and closed her door when he stepped on the elevator. She blinked rapidly for a moment, then shook herself. She should be glad Dallas had apparently accepted her request that they limit their relationship to one of friendship. Now she could go back to Barbourville and devote herself to the goals she had set, knowing she had proven to herself that she could have existed in Dallas' world if circumstances had allowed them to be more than friends.

She just wished all this hadn't left her feeling so terribly empty.

Chapter Thirteen

Dallas had arrived. The sign said so. Barbourville, Tennessee. Population 2,092.

He eased his foot off the brake and glanced at the bare branches of the maples lining Kessler Boulevard. The vegetation had changed drastically since that day in late summer when he'd driven into town dreading the days he would have to spend here.

Now he was back for entirely different reasons, and he didn't dread much of anything except facing Beth Ann. Seeing her, he feared, would be less than pleasant.

He might as well get it over with. It was only three in the afternoon. She should still be in her store, so he would make that his first stop.

165

Considering it was mid-afternoon on a weekday, downtown Barbourville wasn't particularly crowded and he lucked into a parking spot just a few spaces down the street from Beth Ann's Place.

He climbed out of the car and grabbed his leather jacket from the back seat. The temperatures weren't cold in comparison to what he was accustomed to, but a strong breeze sliced between the buildings, dropping the wind chill factor to a degree approaching miserable. He slipped his jacket on, turned the collar up, tucked his chin in, and hurried down the street.

He didn't look up until he was in front of the store. For a second he thought he'd overshot Beth Ann's Place. Then he looked again and realized that this was the right building but the window dressing had certainly changed.

The decorations, which usually consisted of mannequins dressed in seasonal clothing, today featured a variety of art and craft items. Hand-blown glass, pottery, hand-carved wooden bowls and spoons, woven baskets, watercolors on easels, and half a dozen handmade brooms were artfully arranged behind the glass. A memory tickled the back of his mind and then was gone.

He turned toward the door and was relieved to see BETH ANN'S PLACE still emblazoned on the glass. Frowning, he reached for the knob and let himself in.

The usual little bell jingled when he opened the door. The shop was empty of customers, but Beth Ann sat on a tall stool behind the counter. Half a dozen books were spread out around her. She looked up and her eyes widened.

"Dallas! This is a surprise. Why didn't you tell me you were coming to town?"

He paused and looked around. The only clothes he could spot were a few pieced and quilted vests and a couple of ponchos that appeared to be hand woven. Other than that, the store was filled with the same type of items he'd seen in the window, along with some of the rocking chairs like Beth Ann had bought for his screened-in porch.

Next to the chairs were three small tables, obviously made by the same hand, and he immediately decided he wanted to buy at least two of the tables for the cottage.

Suddenly aware that he'd allowed himself to become distracted, he frowned and turned his attention back to Beth Ann. "What's going on here? Where are the clothes you sell and what's all this stuff?"

Beth Ann picked up a bookmark and slipped it into one of the books spread out on the counter, then closed the book and stood. "I'm sorry. I thought I told you I was turning the store into a co-op where the artists can display and sell their wares. I provide the store and do the bookkeeping and the artists pay me a percentage of the profits. It's working out well for all of us."

Dallas felt a flush touching his cheekbones. "I think you did mention the idea you'd had but I didn't know you'd followed through with it."

She moistened her lips. "Like I said, I'm sorry. I guess I forgot to tell you. You've been hard to reach the last few weeks."

"I've been busy."

Beth Ann raised her brows. "Haven't we all? But why are you here now? Is something wrong at Megan's that I don't know about?"

"Everything is fine so far as I know. I haven't talked to Megan since last week."

"Didn't she know you were coming to town either?"

Dallas felt the warmth on his face intensify. He'd been worried about this moment. Probably with good reason. He took a deep breath. "I'm going to answer all of your questions, Beth Ann, but I need to do so in my own way."

She dropped back onto the stool. "Why do I get the feeling I'm not going to like what I'm about to hear?"

Dallas heaved a sigh. "I hope you'll like it

very much. Now, would you please stop asking questions and let me talk?"

She lifted one shoulder in a half-shrug. Her lips thinned, but she nodded. "I won't say another word. Go ahead and talk."

He took another deep breath. "I've sold out in Chicago and I'm moving to Barbourville permanently."

Beth Ann's eyes widened but she didn't say anything for several seconds. When she did speak, her tone reflected her confusion. "You're kidding, right?"

"Does the thought of my living here upset you?"

"Of course not, but the thought of you making all those changes without breathing a word to me—that I find extremely upsetting."

Dallas wanted to go to her, to wrap his arms around her and tell her he was sorry he had upset her. However, judging by the anger springing to life in her eyes, he feared he might come away from the embrace with only one arm rather than the two he had possessed going in.

"I'm sorry I've upset you. I didn't say anything earlier because I was afraid that things wouldn't work out. I couldn't leave Denver and Dayton dangling. They had to bring in another attorney to take over my caseload, and I had to find a buyer for the condo. There was always a chance I wouldn't be able to make everything work." He needed to moisten his lips, but he didn't want her to realize just how nervous he was.

She continued to stare at him, her expression wooden. "And you couldn't have called me, told me what you were trying to do, and said, 'Hey, Beth Ann, here's what I'm trying to do but I'm not sure it will work out?' What? You were afraid I'd get hysterical if your plans fell through?"

"God, no, Beth Ann. I can't believe you would say that." He wished he'd brought something to drink with him. His mouth felt as though it was lined with a chunk of his wool sweater.

She continued to glare at him. "Why do you want to move to Barbourville anyway?"

He shook his head. He wanted to tell her, wanted to explain how he had changed, but he didn't think she was in any mood to listen right now. He shrugged. "I'll tell you another time. Is it okay if I go by and see Trevor?"

"Of course it's okay. Trevor thinks the sun rises and sets in you. He'll be happy to hear about your plans."

He hated that tone in her voice, the thickness that suggested tears lurked just below the surface. "Look, Beth Ann—"

She threw up a hand to shush him, then shook her head so fiercely that her hair flew out of its clips and into her face. He took a step back. "Perhaps I should go."

She turned her back to him. "Perhaps you should."

"I'll see you later then." He paused, waiting, but she didn't speak again. He knew she was hurt and he didn't want to leave her that way. He stepped closer to the counter and his gaze fell on one of the books lying there. "What's this?"

She spun around. Anger still flashed in her eyes. "It's a book, Dallas. It has words in it. I've been reading those words. Now that we've cleared up that little mystery, will you please leave?"

Dallas reached for another book and pulled it closer, turning it so that the title faced him. "This is a textbook."

"Wow! I'm impressed! You should have been a detective instead of an attorney."

Dallas had been an attorney long enough to recognize a diversionary tactic when he heard one, and he knew the proper procedure was to ignore such tactics. "Beth Ann, why do you have textbooks spread out all around you?"

Her face paled, but she immediately raised her chin. "I hardly see what business that is of yours, Mr. Vance."

"You're making some drastic life changes yourself, aren't you? What are you majoring in?"

She murmured something so softly that he

couldn't make out her words. "What did you say?"

She lifted her chin a bit higher. "I said retail merchandising."

"Let me see if I understand this. In addition to changing your store completely, you've also enrolled in college?"

"Just a community college," she said quickly. "One that has a campus nearby."

"A college is a college, Beth Ann. And you didn't say a word to me about it. May I ask why?"

"I, ah, well." Her face flushed as she stumbled to a halt.

Dallas squared his shoulders and took a step back. "In other words, you've made a lot of changes in your life that you chose not to share with me, but you're furious because I didn't tell you what was going on in my life. Sorry, Beth Ann, but friendship should run both ways, a concept you don't appear to understand. Now, I'll respect your wishes and get out of your store."

Dallas marched to the door and jerked it open. He thought for a split second that he heard Beth Ann call out his name, but if she did, the jingling of the bell above the door drowned out the sound of her voice, and he was far too furious to turn around to see.

* * *

Well, Beth Ann admitted to herself while swiping tears from her face, she had messed up her relationship with Dallas once again. What was wrong with her? She was the one who had insisted they remain friends, but, truth be told, a small part of the reason she'd started working so hard to improve her circumstances was because she hoped someday to feel as though she was almost as well educated and sophisticated as Dallas.

She'd known, of course, that by the time she got a college degree and Trevor turned eighteen—in other words, by the time she was free to move away from Barbourville and at the same time feel somewhat equal in status to Dallas—Dallas would very likely have found someone else to love. In fact, she'd figured that was almost certain to be the case.

So she hadn't changed her goals merely because she had fallen so deeply and irrevocably in love with Dallas Vance. She'd done it for herself and for Trevor, so Trevor would have a role model and be more likely to get a college education himself.

Now Dallas had decided to move to Barbourville, and she wasn't sure why. He'd had a fabulous career in Chicago, a beautiful condo, and obviously a busy social life. Why would he give up all of that to move to Barbourville, Tennessee?

And what would he do with himself here anyway? If he planned to open a law office, he'd be at a distinct disadvantage. When people in a small town needed an attorney, they tended to go to someone they'd known since childhood, someone they'd played ball with in high school. It would take years for Dallas to establish a clientele base here.

She'd been an idiot to let him leave. She should have insisted that he tell her exactly what he had in mind for his future. She loved him too much to let him make a mistake like moving to Barbourville and possibly ruining his life. She needed to warn him about what he was getting himself into.

She hurriedly gathered up her books and shoved them into the backpack she carried. She would close the store early and rush home. He had said he was going to see Trevor. Maybe if she hurried, she could catch him at her house and have a serious talk, a talk where she maintained her cool.

She paused and blew her breath out in a long, frustrated sigh. Okay, maybe she wouldn't be able to maintain her cool, but she could at least try for as long as it took to explain the realities of small-town life to Dallas.

She rushed to the rear of the shop, grabbed her coat and gloves off the rack there, and checked to make sure the back door was locked.

Fifteen minutes later, she had walked home and let herself in the side door. She could tell immediately that Dallas wasn't there. Trevor sat alone at the kitchen table with his schoolbooks spread out around him. He looked up with a quick smile when she came through the door.

"Hey Mom, guess what? Mr. Vance is back in town. He stopped by to visit with me for a few minutes. He said he'd see me later."

"Oh?" Beth Ann pulled her coat off and dropped it onto the back of a kitchen chair. "What else did he say?"

"Not much. He seemed in a hurry. Did you know he was coming to town?"

"No, he hadn't told me. Did he say where he was going?"

"No. I figured he was going across the street to see Mrs. McCray and the babies, but I don't know for sure."

Beth Ann walked to the back window and looked out. She could see through the bare branches of the lilac hedge enough to tell that lights were burning in the cottage. She grabbed her coat again.

"I think he's gone to the cottage. I need to talk with him. I'll be back in a little bit."

"Can I go too?"

"Not this time, sweetie. I need to talk to Dallas alone."

"Is something wrong, Mom?"

"No, no. I just need to tell him something, that's all. I'll be back before long."

She hurried out before Trevor could ask any more questions.

The wind had died down a bit but the cold had developed a dampness that cut to the bone. Beth Ann wished she'd taken time to pull on a hat and her gloves, but she settled for shoving her hands into her pockets and pulling her collar up around her neck and ears. She had just started around the end of the lilac hedge when she slammed into Dallas.

He, too, had pulled his collar up and ducked his head. The collision knocked both of them back a step, but Dallas quickly grabbed Beth Ann's shoulders and steadied her.

"Whoa," he said, keeping a grip on her shoulders. "I wasn't expecting to see you home so soon. Did you close early?"

"Yes. I wanted to talk to you. Where are you headed?"

"I was going across the street to visit Megan and the girls, but that can wait. Is something wrong?"

"There might be. Dallas, I want you to tell me why you decided to move to Barbourville."

He frowned. "Right this second?"

"Yes, please. I really need to know how you plan to make a living here."

He shrugged. "It's simple enough, really. The fact is, the time I spent here last fall made me realize that I wanted something different out of life than what I had going on in Chicago. Renovating the cottage gave me a tremendous feeling of accomplishment, and I loved the notion that I was preserving something from the past and giving it a purpose in the present. I've talked to Richard McCray about what I want to do, and he's got a couple of farmhouses in the county lined up for me to buy. I'll renovate them with his input and resell them."

"You don't plan to go into law, then?"

"I figure Barbourville has enough attorneys, and that's not what I want to do now anyway."

Beth Ann heaved a sigh. "Thank goodness. I was going to warn you that going into law here might be a frustrating experience for you. But are you sure that renovating houses will be enough to provide you with a fulfilling life?"

"Actually, no. I was hoping for a bit more."

Beth Ann's heart slammed into overdrive. "What do you mean?"

His grasp on her shoulders tightened. "I won't tell you, Beth Ann, that you're the only reason I'm moving to Barbourville. I'd want to live here even if you never agreed to more than friendship between us. But I warn you that I'm going to spend every minute that we're together telling you how very much I love you and how much I want you to be a part of my life."

His hands slid slowly across her shoulders and down her arms until he could grasp both of her hands in his. He raised first her right hand and then her left, pressing kisses into the palms. Then he lifted his gaze and looked deep into her eyes.

"I adore you, Beth Ann. You're warm and compassionate, brave and determined, bright and funny and beautiful and there's nothing I want more in the world than the right to call you my wife."

To her horror, Beth Ann felt tears welling up in her eyes. Within a second, they had spilled over and slid down her cheeks. Dallas frowned but also he took a step closer. "I don't know why you're crying, Beth Ann, but you'll never convince me that you don't love me too. We're perfect for each other and we belong together. You know that as well as I do."

She sniffed, then pulled her right hand free from his grasp to dig in her coat pocket for a tissue. Once she found it, she wiped the tears from her cheeks and then blew her nose. "I'm crying because you're so wonderful and I'm so unromantic. What kind of woman lets herself get a runny nose when the man she adores is proposing to her."

Dallas laughed out loud and then pulled her into a crushing embrace. "The kind of woman I want to marry, that's who. What do you say? Are you willing to let me be a part of your and Trevor's lives?"

Beth Ann wrapped her arms around Dallas' waist and laid her cheek against the soft leather of his jacket. Never had she dreamed she'd ever be this happy. But there were words that had to be spoken so there'd be no misunderstandings between her and Dallas in the future.

She pulled back and looked into his eyes. "You need to know, Dallas, that I love you too and I want nothing more than to be your wife, but I'll need to continue with my education and I want to keep an interest in Beth Ann's Place. The store is important to me and to the artists who have their work on sale there."

"Of course I want you to continue with both things. I couldn't love you as I do if you weren't so determined to be your own person. I'm just thankful there's room in your heart and in your life for me to fit in as your husband."

A happy glow brightened Beth Ann's eyes. "There's more than enough room for that, Dallas Vance. I'd be delighted to have you as my husband and, in turn, to be your wife."

She stepped into his arms and tilted her head back. He lowered his lips to hers, and Beth Ann closed her eyes, reveling in the joy and excitement his kiss elicited deep within her. Despite the cold, she felt the warmth of love and contentment spreading throughout her body.

Until something wet and extremely cold landed on her cheek.

She pulled back and looked up. "Snow! It's snowing! Oh, look, Dallas. Isn't it beautiful? This is our first snow of the year. Trevor will be so excited. Let's go share all of this news with him."

"You mean about the snow?"

"Well, yes, but more importantly, about our engagement. He's going to be thrilled about both."

Dallas paused and frowned. "Are you sure, Beth Ann? After all, he's had you to himself his entire life. Perhaps he won't be that happy about having to share you with me."

Trevor's voice sounded from behind the hedge. "Oh, don't you worry about that at all, Mr. Vance. I'll be more than happy to have you as part of our family."

Beth Ann backed out of Dallas' arms, then

grabbed his hand and pulled him around the end of the hedge. Trevor stood there, his hands shoved in his jean pockets and snow coating his hair.

"How long have you been standing there, young man?"

Trevor hung his head for a second, then looked up again and smiled a bit sheepishly. "I knew something was wrong when you came home early, Mom, and then I was especially worried when you acted so strange about needing to see Mr. Vance. Since you wouldn't tell me what was going on, I decided to check it out for myself. I figured that if something was wrong, I ought to be old enough now to help you out a little bit."

He turned to Dallas. "I'm sure glad you're moving to Barbourville, Mr. Vance. But I hope you're not expecting us to live in one of those farmhouses you're buying out in the county. After you and Mom marry, would you fix up our house so we can stay right here on Redbud Road?"

Dallas laughed out loud, then turned back to Beth Ann. "What do you say, Beth Ann? Are you up to renovating your house and continuing to live here? We could turn it into the showplace of Barbourville."

Beth Ann chuckled. "Gad, I can feel control slipping through my fingers as we speak. You two are already ganging up on me. And, frankly, I love it."

She slipped her right arm around Dallas' waist, and he draped his arm across her shoulders. She then motioned for Trevor to step to her other side and she wrapped her left arm around him.

They walked as a threesome through the falling snow back to their future home.